GW00854711

Like Ben Lewis, the <del>hero of *Holiday in Happy*</del> *Street*, Jon Blake ha<del>s always been a rebel.</del> Although his earli<del>est ambition was to be</del> Conservative Prime <del>Minister, as a teenager</del> he ran a satirical magazine, refused to attend religious assembly and chose to do Art A level rather than Latin or Greek ("at which point," he says, "they immediately assumed I was a drug addict"). He then went on to drop out of university.

He began writing for teenagers while teaching in Nottingham: "It was the only way I could keep the Youth quiet and stop them treading me into the ground. Rebels make the best audiences because they only listen when they want to. If you speak from the heart, that's where they listen, and if you don't that's where they turn off." Given this view, it's not surprising that his books generally feature characters who challenge authority – particularly when, as in *Holiday in Happy Street*, it's phoney or unreasonable.

Praised by *The Times Educational Supplement* as "an author to look out for; perceptive and with a good ear for teenage talk", Jon Blake has now written several novels and volumes of short stories, as well as a television play, *Direct Action* (1986). Also published as a Walker paperback is *Geoffrey's First*, described by *The Sunday Times* as "a funny and moving love story".

Jon Blake lives in Cardiff.

Also by Jon Blake

Geoffrey's First
Oddly
Trick or Treat
Yatesy's Rap

Showdown (short stories)

HOLIDAY IN HAPPY STREET

JON BLAKE

WALKER BOOKS
LONDON

First published 1989 by Walker Books Ltd
87 Vauxhall Walk, London SE11 5HJ

This edition published 1990

Printed in Great Britain by
Cox and Wyman Ltd, Reading, Berkshire

British Library Cataloguing in Publication Data
Blake, Jon
Holiday in Happy Street.
I. Title
823'.914 [F]
ISBN 0-7445-1755-9

CHAPTER 1

I am on my way to see a hypnotist. Everyone says I am mad. Perhaps they are right. But I've got this mental block, and I've tried everything, but I can't clear it.

My name is Ben Lewis. Ben to my teachers, and Lewis to my mates. My problem started two days ago, in McGooey's Burger House. It doesn't really matter which McGooey's, because they're all the same, aren't they? For the sake of argument, we'll say it's the McGooey's in your town.

We always spend the hols hanging about in McGooey's. Only divs go to Mr Slurpy's. McGooey's is the Original. McGooey's is the one with Fanti Cola. Anyway, the burgers in Mr Slurpy's are 5p more. 5p is 5p, especially if you've only got 10p.

Actually, two days ago, my mum was feeling generous. I had a quid. That meant I had a whole burger to myself, instead of sharing it with the pigs.

"Come on, gi'us a bite!" says Leon, pig number one.

"Get your own."

"We're your mates!" says Jonno, pig number two.

"Yeah, when it suits you."

I take another slobbering mouthful. Leon's brain ticks over.

"Hey, Jonno," he says. "See that film last night?"

"What film?"

"About them two nuns."

"No?"

"You missed a treat, mate. One of 'em had TB, right? She kept coughing up all this stuff – "

Leon checks me. I ignore him.

" – all this blood and snot, and she gobbed it into this dish – "

I shift to the next seat. Leon and Jonno shift after me.

" – and this other nun, right, she got her finger – "

"Shut up, Leon."

Leon comes over innocent. "Wassamatter?"

"You ain't gonna put me off, so save your breath."

"Wha–? What you on about? I'm only telling Jonno about this film!"

"Go on, Lee," says Jonno.

"Where was I? Oh yeah. This other nun, she gets her finger, right, and she dips it in this stuff ... then you see her mouth opening ... and her finger coming up – "

"*Have* the bastard!"

I smack the burger box across the table.

"Cheers, Ben!"

I watch them fill their faces, like a pair of gannets, and I think to myself, I could do without this. We used to have a good time together. Now all they seem to do is take the piss, and steal the food out of my mouth. Wouldn't it be great, I think, just to go away. Somewhere where nobody knows me. Somewhere where people aren't depressed, and aren't looking for someone to take it out on.

By a strange coincidence, right at this moment, my eyes fall on a leaflet, half screwed up on the chair next to me. With one eye on the others, I smoothe it out.

WIN THE HOLIDAY OF A LIFETIME!
AT
HAPPY STREET
BURGER PARADISE

Simply collect
10
cheeseburger
tokens
and complete
the following
poem
in not more
than four lines

A month of non-stop spending and scoffing!

A chance to meet Huey McGooey in person!

"HUEY McGOOEY IS THE FUNNIEST CLOWN..."

Application form overleaf

"What you got there?" says Leon.

"Nothing," I reply, slipping the leaflet into my pocket.

Which brings me back to the hypnotist. You see, I've got these three lines, and I know they're good, and all I need is one more brilliant line to clinch it. But the inspiration has gone, the well is dry, and I'm buggered if I can think of anything. This is the poem so far:

HUEY McGOOEY IS THE FUNNIEST CLOWN,
SEE HIM DROP HIS TROUSERS DOWN;
WITH HIS NOSE SO RED AND HIS BURGERS
SO CHEWY...

It's worse than constipation. I've tried running round the block, I've tried four cups of black coffee, I've even started at A in the dictionary and worked my

9

way through to Q. I'm getting frown-lines like an old grandad. Yesterday a total stranger said, "Cheer up, mate, it may never happen." "That's the trouble," I told him. "It isn't." Actually, I didn't say that at all. I thought it up ten minutes later. I never get the ideas when I need them.

I'll tell you how desperate I've been. I even asked Dad. I never ask Dad anything, except asking for money, and that's a waste of time as well.

"Dad," I go, "I've been given this really stupid English homework."

I read out my poem.

"With his nose so red," I go, "and his burgers so chewy…"

"All made out of kangaroo-ee," says Dad.

Like I said, waste of time.

The hypnotist was Leon's idea. The hypnotist is Leon's uncle. I wouldn't normally believe anything Leon tells me, but the hypnotist's name is The Great Ivanov. Ivanov is also Leon's name. His family were refugees from eastern Europe. Leon says they were fleeing from the Nazis, which is strange, because they arrived in 1948, after the war had ended. My theory is that they *were* Nazis, fleeing from someone else.

All the way to The Great Ivanov's house, Leon is pumping me for information about this poem of mine. He can't understand why I've been set this really stupid English homework and he hasn't. Soon I have constructed an incredible story about Mrs Parker, our English teacher, and how she is doing a study for the government on the imagination of teenagers. I have been chosen as a guinea-pig because so far my compositions show no imagination whatsoever.

It is such a good story that when we arrive at The Great Ivanov's front door, I have completely convinced myself it is true, although Leon still doesn't believe a word.

Leon reaches for the bell and, as he does so, I get a severe attack of the shits.

"Are you sure your uncle knows what he's doing?" I ask Leon.

"Scared of being put under?" sneers Leon.

"No! I'm just scared he won't get me back again. I saw this film once, and this guy spent his whole life eating lemons and thinking they were cakes. No one could understand it, then they found he'd seen this hypnotist – "

"Lewis," says Leon, "my uncle's a professional."

"Yeah, so was the one in the film."

"That was a film, you div! My uncle's real."

Just to prove the point, the door opens and there stands Leon's real uncle, in a blue boiler suit and beret. He is old but obviously fit, with spanners in his pocket and a wary-old-dog look in his eye. He squares up his wire-rim glasses and says, "Hel-lo, Leon," in a German or maybe Russian accent.

"And who is this?" he adds, turning to me.

"This is Ben, Anton."

Leon's uncle looks me over, faintly amused, as if I am not really much cop. There is a hint of cruelty about his face, and a peaked cap would sit quite happily on the top of it. But he is surprisingly friendly, and invites us in for a cup of tea.

The Great Ivanov's back room gives no clues as to his former life. It is plain, and orderly, and slightly threadbare. There is a brown carpet, a colour telly,

11

bowl of fruit on the table, pictures of fruit on the wall, pot-plants and postcards and 3-in-one oil.

The Great Ivanov brings in three mugs of tea, sits with a brisk tug on his trouser-legs, and pulls his arm-chair vigorously towards me.

"So, gentlemen," he says, "shall we begin?"

Again his eyes rove over me, faintly amused. I keep my chin up and try to look cool.

"Ben's scared, Anton," says Leon. "He thinks you'll put him under and won't get him back."

"I do not!"

"Oo, Ben, you liar. You just said it two minutes ago, outside the door."

"I was talking about a film!"

"If you say so, Ben."

Leon smirks. Leon's uncle doesn't. He views me with a tinge of contempt.

"I have been a hypnotist for forty-five years," he says, as if to say that's the end of the argument.

Leon explains about my mental block, then tells me to recite my poem. As there's no point in going ahead unless I do, I mumble out the lines as quickly as possible, with my eyes fixed firmly on the ceiling. When I lower them again, The Great Ivanov is dangling a silver locket from finger and thumb.

"Do exactly as I say," he commands.

It is hard to take it seriously as he begins swinging the locket. I have seen this kind of thing so many times that I half expect to hear Vincent Price saying, "You are getting sleeee-py." Nevertheless I keep my eyes on the locket and The Great Ivanov says nothing about getting sleepy, just tells me to concentrate. His voice is very soft and reasonable and I begin to feel

12

like a baby. To and fro goes the locket, to and fro, till I am going to and fro as well, and the voice becomes like a distant call on a summer beach. Vaguely I am aware that I am going under, that there is no need to fight it, that my troubles and cares are melting away...

Then CLICK!

"What happened?" I blurt.

Leon laughs.

"Am I under?" I ask.

Leon folds gently in two, the laughter now painful.

"Just tell me, am I awake, or am I under? I don't know what's going on!"

Terrifying thoughts race through my mind. I'm dead. They've given me drugs. I've gone mad. My hand claws into the chair, desperate for something real.

"Excellent poem, my friend," says Leon's uncle.

There is something different about him. He sits back with his arms folded, same clothes, same face, but different.

"What did I say?" I ask him.

"You said, 'The funniest clown, is Huey McGooey'."

At first hearing, this doesn't sound too impressive. But I think about it. Mrs Parker has a motto which is Simple Is Best. Perhaps she is right. Perhaps all along I have been looking for something incredibly clever, when really I should have gone for something obvious.

I try it out in my head.

HUEY McGOOEY IS THE FUNNIEST CLOWN,

13

SEE HIM DROP HIS TROUSERS DOWN;
WITH HIS NOSE SO RED AND HIS BURGERS
SO CHEWY,
THE FUNNIEST CLOWN IS HUEY McGOOEY.

"Do you think it'll win?" I ask The Great Ivanov.

"Win what?" says Leon.

Leon and his uncle bear in on me with quizzical expressions. I blunder and burble and do not make a lot of sense.

"Save your breath," says Leon. "We know about Happy Street."

I'm dumbstruck. What else have I told them? God, I've got so many secrets! I want to grab Leon by the throat and force him to tell me what he's found out. But I decide I'd rather not know.

When I arrive home from The Great Ivanov's, I have another strange experience. Mum is standing at the gate, chatting to Mrs Foster. She casts an anxious eye over a ketchup stain on my shirt. Meanwhile I am watching her in a kind of stupefied trance. Who is she? I mean, I know who she is, but who is she? Everything seems different since visiting Leon's uncle. It's like I've been born again, and everything familiar is suddenly strange, and the strangest thing of all is that I am so confident. There is one answer missing on the crossword, and I never can answer crosswords, but I take one look and fill it straight in. And the moment my competition entry drops with a little soft clunk in the postbox, I start planning what clothes to pack. There is no doubt whatever that my name is on that holiday.

14

For two days I sit motionless in an armchair, sniffing at the little wafting smells, like a rodent. I have no desire to go out, no desire to watch TV, no desire to do anything but wait.

On the third day, Mum calls me into the hall. There is a sky-blue envelope on the mat. It is addressed to me. On the back is printed McGOOEY INTERNATIONAL.

Very calmly, I tear open the envelope and read the contents.

"Better pack my case," I tell Mum. "I've just won first prize."

CHAPTER 2

All right. I know it seems too good to be true. But when you are sitting in your own private railway carriage, with a free quarter pounder in front of you, and a month of luxury up ahead, you do not ask questions. You say thanks very much.

For the tenth time, I count out the Smiley Tokens I have to spend. There are supposed to be fifty, but each one has got one thousand marked on it. I wonder if someone's made a mistake, and they've given me fifty thousand. If so, I suppose I ought to be honest and tell them. On the other hand, McGooey is one of the twenty largest companies in the world, with interests in food, leisure, banking and art treasures. It can afford a few quid.

I sit back, relax, and watch the scenery go by. All the familiar landmarks are way behind me, along with school, Mum and Dad, Leon and Jonno, and all my other tedious problems. Mum says I'll be back in a week. That's just what she wants to think.

We enter a long, long tunnel. The train almost seems to be travelling in circles, spiralling down and down and finally out into the blinding sun, at which point the engine cuts off, and for a while we cruise silently, while I pray nothing has gone wrong.

It has all been planned. Where there was silence there is the sudden beating of syn-drums, gradually growing louder. We reach a sign saying Happy Street Halt. My adrenalin surges. Next second I see the first of the drummers, beating sturdily on a big black elec-

16

tronic drum kit. He is followed by another, then another, then another. There are a dozen drummers, all in perfect synch, beating down like a mighty rain. A bum-thumping bass rises from the earth, then the iron throat of fifty chunking reggae guitars. Suddenly there are people everywhere, dancing, chasing, hand-clapping, tipping back bottles of Fanti Cola. Horns ring out, and high above me I see the swinging feet of the trumpeters on the station roof. As if to advertise the many delights of Happy Street, there are people in ski-outfits, carnival costumes, skating suits and disco dress. Many are waving and, as the train pulls to a halt, the waving becomes almost frantically excited.

It is only when I take my first step on to the platform that I realize who they are waving at. I am the only person getting off.

A train guard hurries through and takes my luggage. A voice from the crowd says, "Ben, isn't it?"

A family separate themselves, and stand before me, beaming. It is the woman who has spoken to me. She is about thirty, with a mane of fair hair, high forehead, unblinking eyes, and a small, well-controlled smile. At first sight she seems casually, almost sloppily dressed, then you notice the expensive leather belt on her jeans, and the little gold wristwatch, and the designer label on her floppy shirt.

The woman's arm is round a man roughly twice her age. He has neat silver hair, a bulbous nose, a double chin and laughing eyes. He wears a smart blue suit and on the lapel is a badge featuring a colour photo of the same silver hair, bulbous nose, etc. Energy, confidence and importance seep from every inch of him, like a great kindly uncle who also happens to be president of the world.

The man's hands rest on the shoulders of twin girls, with braided hair, matching silver tracksuits and faces as eager as our Patch at walkies-time.

"I'm Tish," says the woman, in a warm, husky, plummy voice.

I shake her hand, which is light and weak.

"And I," says the man, in a gushing, walnutty voice, "am DT."

He pumps my hand furiously, with a big knowing wink.

"I'm Alice," says the first girl, confidently. "I did love your poem, Ben."

"Oh... thanks."

"And I'm Hattie," says the second, rather more coyly. "Call me Hat if you like."

"All right."

"So Ben," says Alice, taking me by the arm. "Is it Ben, or would you prefer Benjamin? Names are so important, don't you think? Now, let me show you the street."

"Alice," says Hattie, starting a small tug-of-war with me, "I'm going to show Ben the street."

"Wo-wo-wo!" says DT, holding up both hands, chuckling. "Young ladies! Ben's had one heck of a journey. How about letting him settle in?"

Alice and Hattie instantly let go. Alice claps a hand to her face, while Hattie puts on a little-girl-sorry expression.

"Of course!" says Alice.

"Super sorry, Ben," says Hattie, making big cow-eyes at me.

"I'm sure Ben will have plenty of time for you

later," says Tish. "Now run along."

The girls flash a farewell smile, then run off, giggling, with a large hula-hoop.

"Kids!" says DT, shaking his head.

"Love 'em," says Tish.

"Now come on, Ben," says DT, laying a hand on my shoulder and leading me down the platform. "Let's sort you out with some quarters. Then maybe you and I can have a good game of pool. Like pool, young man?"

"Never played it."

"Get along with you!" says DT, laughing and slapping me on the back. "You love it!"

CHAPTER 3

Dear Mum + Dad
 Arrived safely. Weather
sunny. Everybody friendly.
They have given me my
own hut with a shower
and phone and a stereo.
It is almost too good to
be true.
 I'm not homesick, so
there.
 Love from Ben.

Mr + Mrs Lewis
137 Goldacre
Milton Keynes
Bucks
ENGLAND

You don't have to buy postcards on Happy Street.
There is a little stack of them on the desk. My hut is
full of homely touches like that. A picture of Huey
McGooey hangs on the wall, and beside the bed there
is a black book which says *History of McGooey
International Vols I - IV*.

I am just leafing through this book when there is a
knock at the door. *My* door. Before I have a chance to
answer it, Alice and Hattie come waltzing in. I don't
like to say anything, because maybe that's the way
things are on Happy Street.

"Hiya, Ben!" says Alice.

"Everything OK, Ben?" says Hattie.

"Great, thanks."

I notice that Alice and Hattie have changed outfits
since an hour ago. Now they wear grandad shirts,
denim skirts and ski pants underneath. They wander
about the room as if we are old friends, investigating
this and that. Alice reads out my postcard, and they

say "Ah!" and ask me why I haven't put kisses on the bottom, because I *must* love my mum, and she *must* miss me terribly. Before I can reply, Hattie has taken the book out of my hands and placed it religiously on the bedside table.

"Now, you must look after this," she says.

"Why did they give it to me?" I ask.

"There's one in every room," says Alice.

"Have I got to read it?" I ask.

They giggle.

"You haven't *got* to do anything!" says Alice.

"Happy Street is the Street of Freedom," says Alice, as if reciting a poem learnt long ago.

"Now come on, Ben," says Hattie, tugging me by the hand. "You simply *must* see Happy Street."

"Shall we roller-skate, or take a fun buggy?" says Alice.

The fun buggies are parked in the courtyard outside. There are all different types, some like overgrown toy tractors, some like pleasure-boats on wheels, with hoops of coloured neon going over. They could have been made from an outsize Lego kit, with big blue batteries underneath, and all the workings showing.

I wander round the one that takes my fancy, hardly daring to touch.

"Can anyone drive them?" I ask.

"Of *course*," says Alice.

The girls scramble into the back. Doubtfully I sink down behind the wheel. You sit low, almost to the ground, with a panel of gauges like Concorde in front of you. Nervously I turn the *START* key. There is a musical hum, the neon flickers on and a friendly computer voice says, "Just great, Ben. You're doing just great. Now press gently on the orange foot pedal."

I press down and off we go. Of course, I have no idea how to drive a fun buggy, but the computer voice gives all kinds of hints and tips without being too pushy. And besides, the fun buggy has bumpers like a dodgem, and it is quite all right to bang into trees and walls and anything else in the way. In fact, it seems preferable to have as many accidents as possible. I soon came across other buggies banging into everything in sight and even each other, which only makes everybody laugh and exchange phone numbers.

As I turn the corner into Happy Street itself, I realize why the fun buggies have to be so safe. There are hundreds, weaving up and down, along a street that stretches for evermore. It is like no other street in the world. Everything – road, lamp-posts, benches, buildings – is made out of sandstone, sandstone all the colours of the rainbow. Pastel greens, cool blues, sun yellows, colours you can't believe came out of nature. But this is McGooey's, so you know there can't be any artificial ingredients.

I slow to a crawl. Every few yards a new smell drifts into my face – hot donut oil, wood-smoke, honeysuckle, sea air. No two buildings are the same. They all stand separate, some cosy as cottages, some powerful as skyscrapers, but they all magically fit together like a happy family coming together for Christmas. Running down both sides of the road are high trees, with wonky white trunks that wander right up into the sky, then spread out into a deep green canopy that roofs in the whole of Happy Street, letting the sunlight through like brilliant streamers.

Across the street, at regular intervals, are the flags of all nations, and beaming portraits of Huey McGooey, painted by little children. Beneath each row of flags is something new. A crazy ice rink, a mint-green swimming pool, stalls hanging in mid-air selling endless records and clothes. And everywhere people: none old, none ugly and none like teachers.

The only problem is, I can't decide where to go first. My eyes flit hungrily between the Dallas Fantasy Building, the Pop Video Supermart, the Museum of the Princesses and Fighter Planes, the Circular Screen Quad-sound Cinema and the Fame School of Art, Dance, Drama and Being Somebody. And that's only one side of the street.

"You really can do *anything*?" I ask Alice and Hattie.

"Happy Street is the Street of Freedom," they chorus together.

"But I don't know where to start."

Alice and Hattie wear expressions of motherly concern, well beyond their twelve years of age.

"I know it's tough, Ben," says Hattie. "It was tough for us at first."

"Seeing as it's your first day," says Alice, "let's head straight for the Burger Cathedral."

"That's a great idea, Alice," says Hattie.

"Do you think?"

"Really I do."

"Well thank you. It's generous of you to say."

"Well thank you."

Anyone who couldn't see Alice and Hattie's faces might think they are taking the piss. But I swear they

23

were utterly sincere. I begin to wonder if they've got some hidden script they're reading from. Maybe this is how everybody acts after they've been on Happy Street a while.

We drive down Happy Street, the whole length of it, till we reach a great arch in the shape of a Fanti Cola bottle. It is known as the Fanti Arch, and it is the meeting place for all the young people on Happy Street. They swap phone numbers and stamps and teach each other Fanti Cola songs in their own language, because every nation on Earth is represented.

We glide beneath the arch, waving back at the kids. The road opens out into a great courtyard of multicoloured pebbles, and I catch my first breathtaking glimpse of the Burger Cathedral.

Imagine the greatest building you have ever seen, and the Burger Cathedral will make it look like a tin shack. The Taj Mahal, the Empire State, St Paul's, they're nowhere! The Cathedral sits over Happy Street like a galactic mother hen, with towers at each corner taller than mountains, shaped like giant double-cornets. Between them the building rises through stripes of stone of every colour, like slices of some mouthwatering cake, towards an astronomic dome, like a second moon fallen to Earth. From the ground to the summit run towering windows of shivering gold glass, and through the glass there are glimpses of exotic trees, and cascading waterfalls of silver coins, and laser fires, though nothing is exactly clear, like that feeling you sometimes get, that feeling of wanting something, but not knowing what, something so exquisite and perfect you can never quite grasp what it is.

"Ben?" says Alice, quietly.

I turn, dazed.

"Would you put this on, please?"

She hands me a red cape and a McGooey baseball Blitzer Cap.

"It's the done thing," whispers Hattie, who's already wearing hers.

There is no door to the Burger Cathedral. We enter by a glass escalator, which curves in a great sweep across the front of the building, then seems to melt into the walls, like entering another dimension. Every smell I've smelled on Happy Street seems to hit me at once. The interior opens out before us, like a great truth suddenly revealed, and there at the summit of the escalator is none other than the most popular figure in the entire world, Huey McGooey himself.

My eyes fog and my legs go weak. I must have seen him a thousand times, with his chessboard suit and his painted smile and his cherry-red nose. But that was telly. This is real.

"My friend," he says. "At last we meet."

I look behind me. Just Alice and Hattie. I turn back to see Huey McGooey holding my competition entry before him and reciting it in the manner of a great Shakespeare play.

"Let me shake the hand of the man who wrote those lines!"

I quickly wipe my hand, even though I washed it half an hour ago. Huey McGooey grasps it and gives me the secret Fanti Club handshake, with a knowing wink.

"And have you brought my egg, Mr Ben?" he says.

My face falls. "What egg?"

25

"Ah. Now I see."

Huey McGooey reaches behind my ear, and suddenly there is a large brown egg in his hand. He holds it between finger and thumb, then rolls it in his palms and in a flash it is gone and a white dove is fluttering up into the roof.

"Now, young man," he says, and puts a forefinger under my chin. "What do I see here?"

He tut-tut-tuts.

"What a handsome young face," he says. "Such a shame to spoil it with a frown."

"It's from thinking too hard," I tell him.

"Simpson?" says Huey McGooey, clicking his fingers at his assistant. "One kingburger epic for my young friend. And a double-cream raspberry creamshake."

Simpson hurries off with the order.

"Now tell me," says Huey, "what has a lucky young lad like you got to frown about?"

I lick my lips and smile, as big and broad as the grin painted on Huey's own face.

It is only after ten minutes of gazing up into the Cathedral dome that I realize what I am looking at. It is the top half of a burger bun, on an epic scale. Immediately everything else falls into place. The soft, lumpy floor beneath me represents a giant burger. And the people, all in their red caps and capes, are the relish.

I can't say it was ever my ambition to be a lump of tomato. Yet I've never felt better. It's like being part of an army. More than that. It's like being part of a legend. The McGooey legend. The beefburger that conquered the world.

The servery is the altar of the Cathedral. Behind it, staff work furiously to keep the fifty burgers a minute sliding down the chutes. The whole area is lit by the violet neon lights of the insect-o-cutors, and there are homely little touches like the sign which reads: YOU DON'T HAVE TO BE MAD TO WORK HERE, BUT IT HELPS.

Soon I am settling down, with Alice and Hattie opposite, and a kingburger, fries, creamshake and cola piled up like a barricade between us. I sink my teeth into the full half-pounder, like a lion into its prey. It oozes with juices and relish, which squirt over both cheeks and drip off my chin. I am out there on the wild frontier, with the camp fires blazing and the grunts of the cowboys pumping iron. Hairs spring from my chest with every mouthful.

Now for the cola. The can fits snugly into my fist, like a hand grenade. I rip out the pin, tip back my head and drink like a pirate. I'm drinking the taste of success.

BURRRRRP!

No sooner have I finished than a waitress hurries up and removes the wreckage. I'd like to say I feel satisfied, but somehow you always want more, even when you're full to bursting.

Alice and Hattie are slumped against each other, like victims of some minor disaster, with streaks of mayonnaise down their capes. My eyes wander past them, to the far side of the Cathedral. That side is open, with tables going out on to some kind of patio, like the relish squirting out of the bun. I glimpse blue sky and a seagull flying past. I just *know* there'll be something good out there.

I struggle to my feet, say goodbye to the girls, and explore. I am not disappointed. To my amazement, the patio is perched right on the edge of a high, high cliff, looking out over a monstrous ocean, with islands dotted here and there, and crumbling forts on the islands and music-and-light shows pulsing from the forts. The lights and the sunset turn the whole sky into a theatre and the audience into insects.

"Hey there! Ben!"

DT is sitting with Tish at a nearby table.

"Come and join us!" says Tish.

I sit with them. Tish has changed into a red silk evening dress. There are candles on the table and endless red bottles, mostly empty. A warm breeze flutters the tablecloth. DT covers Tish's hand with a big priestly paw.

"It's our anniversary," says DT. "I've been married twenty-nine years."

"Yes, and I've been married two," says Tish.

"I always marry on the same day," says DT. "That way, I never forget the card. Just the name."

"Oh, DT!" says Tish, flapping weakly at his arm.

Tish and DT tell me all about their wonderful marriage, and how they've never had one cross word, and how they hope that one day I too will be as happy. Tish says that DT is the most romantic man she has ever met, and the most caring, kind, generous and amusing. DT laughs and says he is just an old fart really. Tish insists passionately that he is *not* old, and not one of those other things either.

I like DT. He's like one of those teachers you can have a laugh with, but only because they're so much in control. He's a kind of modern-day cavalier. He treats life as if it's one big feast, there to be enjoyed. I wish my dad was like DT, instead of being all small and careworn and scared to put one foot in front of the other. I love the way DT can just lay hands on everybody. He even lays hands on the waitress's forearm as he whispers, "Get us another bottle, will you, my dear?"

Tish wants to know all about me, from my favourite subjects to my favourite colour socks. She is so interested and amused by everything I say that soon I am almost convinced that I really am interesting and amusing. I tell her all the jokes that I've heard at school and she laughs at every one, often well before I reach the punchline. I introduce a few arm movements and funny voices, things I'd never do at home. Tish loves it all. When DT starts up, Tish turns back to face him instead, and I feel the smallest pang of jealousy. But I notice that now and then her attention strays and her eyes rove efficiently over another woman's hairdo or jewellery. Then she realizes that DT has made a joke, and out comes this absent-minded smile, and a squeeze of his hand, and another petite sip from the glass of red stuff before her.

DT notices I am not drinking. He offers me a glass of the same red stuff.

"Oh no, darling – " starts Tish.

"What's that?"

"Ben's rather young for Happy Juice, don't you think?" says Tish, none too certainly.

"Of course," says DT. "You are absolutely right, my darling. As always."

Tish smiles gratefully. I'm not so pleased myself.

"Sorry, Ben, but Her Word is Law," says DT, pouring me a mug of Fanti Cola.

"You see who wears the trousers around here," he adds, with a nudge.

"Oh, DT, really!" says Tish.

There is a lull in the conversation. Once again I am engrossed by the crumbling forts, and epic sky, and endless sea. There must be a way down there, on to the beach. I know it's late, but this is a holiday, and no holiday is complete without a beach.

"Can you get down from here?" I ask.

"Down?" says DT, slightly surprised. "Down where?"

"To the beach."

"Oh, the beach. No, there's no way down from here."

"How do I get down?"

DT and Tish exchange glances.

"The view's much better from up here, Ben," says Tish.

"Yeah, but I want to get down."

Tish seems a little concerned. "I'm sorry, Ben. I don't follow you."

"It's not the same, just looking," I explain. "I want to be there."

Tish still can't grasp what I'm saying.

"Ben," says DT, sympathetically, "there are a thousand things to do on the street. Things you may never get the chance to do again. You can go to the beach any day of your life."

"I can't. I live in Milton Keynes."

There is a pause.

"Will you take me down?" I plead.

DT and Tish exchange another glance.

"Tomorrow, maybe," says Tish.

DT bangs the table with the flats of his hands and gets up, chuckling.

"Questions, questions, questions!" he says. "Say, how about that game of pool we were going to have?"

CHAPTER 4

In the morning I am woken by a tappety-tap-tap at the door. A woman's face appears. It is a fat face, with rosy cheeks and a spotted duster tied round the top.

"Can I do you now, young sir?" she says.

"What time is it?"

"That's not for me to say, my love," she says, struggling in with a metal bucket, mop, feather duster, polish and broom. "If you want to know the time, ask a policeman."

I peer at my alarm. Seven a.m. The strange cleaning woman dusts busily round the room, picks up my dirty socks, shakes out the mat, and pays religious attention to the portrait of Huey McGooey. As she does so, she begins to sing:

"He is the rock
And our solid found–ation!
He is the rock
We build our lives up–on!"

Just as she reaches the sink, I remember I was sick in it last night. I curl under the duvet in embarrassment.

"Oo, my Gawd," she says. "Been taken poorly, love?"

"Too much Fanti Cola."

"Oo, you poor old soul. And no mum to look after you."

There is a quiet *plink!* and a fizz. When I look up, the cleaning woman is standing over me with what looks like a glass of dentist's mouthwash.

"This'll sort you out," she says.

She pushes the glass into my hand. I sip it nervously. It tastes like cherry and sherbet with a hint of turkish delight.

"Call me Mrs D," says the woman, warmly.

"Thank you, Mrs D."

Mrs D takes the glass, straightens the duvet, and flicks my fringe across.

"Boys," she says. "Helpless without their mums."

Soon she is working away at the sink, with vigorous elbows and vast squirts of liquid Ajax. She gives the toilet bowl a going-over for good measure, then dusts lovingly over the cover of *History of McGooey International, Vols I - IV*, whistling the song she's sung before. "Boys!" she says, clearing up the rubbish I've left over the floor. "Boys!" she says again, almost angrily, as she bangs the leg of the chair back into place. "Love 'em!" she says, as she collects up her things, waves a feather duster in the air, and struggles out.

It feels like the day after Christmas when I walk out again on to Happy Street. I've got that second wind of excitement, finding that all the presents are still there, and somehow even more fresh, and more real, and a whole new day of cola-glugging to look forward to.

Even at seven-thirty, Happy Street is buzzing. All the stores are open. Maybe they never shut. I wander around a few, asking if anyone has seen Tish or DT. Everyone knows DT because DT is on the Board. The Board meet in the Dallas Fantasy Building. But no one knows exactly where DT is right now. I'm directed to the Police Station.

The Police Station doesn't look like a Police Station at all. It looks more like a filling station, with a forecourt and a row of Info machines like petrol pumps and a swinging sign saying *WELCOME*. Where the shop might be there is a white concrete chalet, as solid as a rock, with joke shell-holes all over it and a blue lamp above the door. On the lamp it says *LAUGHING POLICE*.

I walk in. The inside of the chalet is like an old-fashioned sweet shop with a carved wooden counter and a brass bell. I ring the bell. A curtain rustles. Out comes a tall policeman with a handlebar moustache and a tie with little cricketers all over.

"Can I help you, sir?" he says, in a warm, oaky voice.

"I'm looking for DT."

"I'm afraid you won't find him here, sir."

"Sorry to bother you."

"That's perfectly all right, sir. The kettle's just boiled. How about a nice cup of cha?"

The policeman lifts the flap on the counter. I go through.

"Excellent poem, sir, if you don't mind me saying," he whispers, as I pass him.

"Oh, thanks."

"We like a bit of poetry, here at the station."

The policeman moves the curtain aside. I find myself in a cosy back room, just like my nan's, except there is a portrait of Huey instead of the Queen. A second policeman is gently rocking in a rocking-chair, next to an antique leather-top desk. On the desk is an Old English Sheepdog, peering nervously over the edge.

"Any luck, Bosun?" says the handlebar policeman.

"Not a whit, Admiral," says the other, lightly prodding the sheepdog with a biro.

"This young chappie could do with a cup of cha," says the handlebar policeman.

"Pleased to meet you, sir," says the other, offering a hand. "Bosun Barnes at your service."

I shake his hand, which is moist and cold and flimsy. I don't suppose he's twenty, but his hair is thinning and he is pale and scrubbed-over like an old log on a beach.

"And I am Admiral Atkins," says the handlebar policeman.

I shake his hand, which is dry and leathery and slightly painful. His face is leathery too, with flat-top eyes and slightly rotten teeth.

Bosun Barnes stirs a large brown teapot, then warms his hands on it.

"Excuse me," I ask him, "but why is that dog on the table?"

"Flossie here?" says the Bosun. "We're teaching the silly blighter to pounce."

"Best nose I've seen on a dog," says the Admiral, "but darn me if the blessed thing will pounce."

Bosun rattles a tin marked *SWEAR BOX* in the Admiral's face.

"What's that for?" says the Admiral. "I only said 'blessed'."

"Sorry, Admiral," says the Bosun. "I thought you said 'blooming'."

"Why don't you get an Alsatian?" I ask them.

The two policemen wince as if I've just scraped a

shovel on concrete.

"Oo, no," says Admiral. "Wrong image altogether."

"Yes, but they catch criminals," I say.

The policemen's mouths drop open. The Admiral splutters. The Bosun lets out a full-blooded laugh. Soon the two of them are doubled up, laughing and laughing, laughing fit to bust.

"Well bless my cotton socks!" says the Admiral. "There are no criminals on Happy Street!"

"Then why are there policemen?" I ask, slightly miffed.

Gradually they calm down and dry their eyes. The Admiral looks at me just like Mr Channon does when I've asked how to spell something which is already on the blackboard.

"What do you *normally* have policemen for?" he asks.

I so desperately don't want to look stupid, my mind is a total blank.

"To tell the time!" answers the Bosun.

"To give directions!" says the Admiral.

"But most of all..." they chime together, "to laugh!"

They're off again. Holding their sides, wiping their eyes, laughing and laughing, till I can't help myself, and I'm laughing along with them.

"Oh dear, oh dear, oh dear," says the Admiral. "Let's have that cup of cha, Bosun. This young feller'll be the death of me."

The Bosun pours the tea, three cups, and a saucer for Flossie. We sit quietly stirring, in a warm after-laugh glow.

"I've just thought of something," I say.

"Fire away," says the Admiral.

"Could you direct me to the beach?"

I seem to have set them a real poser.

"The beach," says the Admiral, rubbing his chin. "Now then…"

"The beach," says the Bosun, drumming his biro. "Hmmm…"

Suddenly the Admiral downs his tea and jumps to his feet.

"Come along then, sir," he says. "If it's the beach you want, the beach you shall have."

It's cool to walk down Happy Street with the Bosun and the Admiral. Everyone knows them. They have a word with one woman about her cat's operation, and give a tip to another about her flowering shrubs. They offer directions here, directions there, and even tell the time to people who haven't asked. After half an hour we've made about fifty yards. But no one's in any hurry on Happy Street, except me, it seems.

Suddenly the Admiral stops in his tracks and salutes.

"There you go, sir."

I look about, well confused. "This isn't the beach."

"Beach?" says the Admiral.

"We thought you said the Fame School of Art, Dance, Drama and Being Somebody," says the Bosun.

"You must learn to express yourself more clearly," says the Admiral.

"In which case," says the Bosun, "the Fame School is just the place for you."

The Admiral holds open the door. I hesitate.

"Don't you want to be Somebody?" says the Admiral.

"Well ... yeah."

They relax. "There you go then, sir," says the Bosun, helping me in. "Lottie Van Broadway will sort you out, or I'm a Chinaman."

The two policemen retreat, well pleased with themselves, while I study a sign saying *TO BE SOMEBODY*. I follow the arrow into a long, broad corridor. Immediately I am swept up in a stampede of kids, hundreds of them fighting to get their hands highest in the air as they tear at breakneck speed towards the door at the far end. I crouch away, but the stampede goes on and on. At last I'm left alone, but not entirely alone, because the whole corridor is festooned with leaflets and posters advertising a thousand different stage shows and variety acts and bands and books, all struggling for space in a suffocating forest of paper. Slightly dazed, and grateful to be alive, I follow the corridor into an even longer corridor full of old props and burnt-out amps, and lifesize puppets with legs splayed and heads hanging. At the end of this corridor is a door marked *THE THEATRE*. I open it. I am in an old-fashioned school hall, with a high stage at the far end. A dozen kids are on the stage, formed into a conga, in front of a backdrop of skyscrapers and *NEW YORK, NEW YORK* in giant gold letters. The kids bunny-hop from one side to the other while a tiny red-haired woman bashes dramatically at a grand piano. They burst into song:

> "I'll sing like a silly quacky duck,
> I'll dance like a panto horse,

I'll dress in fur like a pussy cat,
I'll do anything for applause!"

They jump to the front, drop on to one knee, and throw out their arms.

"Applause! Applause!
Oh won't you give me yours?
Applause! Applause!
I'll do anything for applause!"

They finish with a great waving of hands. There is a deafening silence. The kids bow and curtsy and blow kisses to the empty hall.

"Bella," says the red-haired woman. "Darling. Why are you at the front? Dimples, Bella! So let's see them, shall we? Big, big smile! And press your finger into your cheek, we've been over this a thousand times!"

"Oh heavens!" cries a small boy, clutching his head.

"Redgrave, dear, whatever is the matter?"

"My shoelace!" cries the boy. "It's broken!"

All the other kids take it in turns to have a disaster like Redgrave's. They rush about the stage, clutching their heads, shrieking *HEAVENS* and *GOOD GRIEF* and *OH MY GIDDY AUNT*. In the middle of the mayhem, the woman swings round on her piano stool to face me.

"And do you wish to join us, my dear?"

Silence. The disasters are suddenly forgotten. I am the focus of all interest.

"Name, dear?"

"Ben."

"Ben!" says the woman, as if I've just solved the Meaning of Life. "His name is Ben, everybody!"

39

The room erupts into applause. I begin to wonder if I really have done something clever. The woman clutches her hands together.

"Isn't that a lovely sound, Ben?"

"Yes."

"Well, Ben. My name is Lottie Van Broadway. You may call me Miss Van Broadway."

"Thank you."

"So, Ben. Will you join us?"

"Yes, join us, Ben!" cries the dimple girl, and all the rest chime in behind: "Join us, Ben!" "*Do* join us, Ben!" "You'll love it, Ben." "We're a crazy bunch, Ben!"

"Actually," I say, "I think I'm in the wrong room."

There is a huge moan, and I almost take it back.

Redgrave and another boy called Oliver lead me down the corridors towards the Art Room. That's what I told them I was looking for. They demonstrate how to sword-fight, and juggle, and do impressions of Donald Duck.

"Do you know 'Maria' from *West Side Story*?" asks Redgrave, and sings it anyway, with Oliver doing the ballet steps. With great effort I manage to shut them up and get them to stand still.

"Do you know the way to the beach?" I ask them.

They pull big-surprised faces.

"'The Way to the Beach'?" says Redgrave.

"Isn't that from *Jesus Christ Superstar*?" says Oliver.

Without warning they are off again, in a dramatic ballet, singing at the top of their voices:

"The way to the beach!

The way to the beach!"

They fight for the centre of the corridor, trying to outdo each other.

Redgrave puts a hand across Oliver's mouth.

"I'm auditioning for Judas!" says Redgrave.

"Oh, *I* want that part!" says Oliver.

"Everybody wants it," says Redgrave. "Everybody in the whole wide world."

"Why don't you audition for Jesus?" says Oliver. "You'd make a *super* Jesus, Redgrave."

"Oh, I don't know, Oliver," says Redgrave. "Why is it that the *bad* parts are so much better than the *good* parts?"

We have reached a door saying *ART ROOM*. Redgrave and Oliver formally introduce me to the doorhandle and insist that I say "Hello, doorhandle". They clap furiously, then dance back down the corridor, arm in arm, singing "I don't know how to love him".

I knock gently and walk in. It is a beautiful room, spacy and circular and filled with light, almost like a chapel. There is a single designer pot of yellow sunflowers on a pale blue marble plinth, and easels set up all round, like the numbers on the face of a clock. All is quiet and holy and still, apart from the gentle flick of brushes.

A man in a blue smock, with a walrussy face approaches. He tells me his name is Stefan, then inspects my hands. He is delighted with them. He says they are an artist's hands. I stare at them in amazement. Stefan guides me to an easel and hands me a real palette of paint, oil paint, not those cheap squeezy bottles of poster paint that Mrs Langham

41

gives us.

Time hardly exists in the Art Room. I dab peacefully at my canvas, in the slow sleepy sun, exchanging the occasional smile with another artist. No one knocks over my paint, no one flicks water at me, and no one says, "What's that meant to be, Lewis?" The only words I get are words of encouragement and advice from Stefan. He is especially keen that I keep my colours bright and clean and sunny, and paint everything as exactly as possible, so that all the other people on Happy Street will be able to understand it. Gradually Stefan convinces me that I am creating a work of true genius, and the more he says it, the more I see it myself.

Then disaster strikes. My brush shoots up the canvas putting a smear of green straight through the yellow. The reason for this is a sudden *crash* at the Art Room door. A girl has come in, about sixteen, with flat cap, baggy tramp's trousers, and paint-spattered boots. In a flash, Stefan is across the room, struggling to push her back out. She strains against him, almost in tears. With ruthless efficiency he manhandles her through the door and into the corridor, while she screams abuse into his face.

I look round at the other artists. Quickly their eyes dart back to their canvasses. Soon they are painting again, while the scuffling and bawling goes on, hardly a yard from the door. The woman next to me asks politely if she can borrow one of my brushes. I am so amazed that I hand it to her without hesitation. All the while, my heart is going BE-BANG BE-BANG BE-BANG BE-BANG.

I tell myself that it's nothing to do with me, and try

to copy everyone else's attitude. But it's no good, because I can still hear them, and I have just got to know what is going on. I decide to pretend I need the toilet.

Out in the corridor, Stefan is screening the girl, talking very quietly and reasonably to her. As I pass she yells "Don't touch me!" and pulls her arm away from him. I catch a glimpse of her face, with mouth hanging open and rubbery lip quivering. If looks could kill, Stefan would be dead ten times over.

I slip into the toilet, run a tap, and put my ear to the door. The girl is calling Stefan an idiot. He's taking it pretty well, considering. She practically orders him to let her in to the Art class. He tells her that she's been given her chance, time and again, and time and again she's blown it. Someone else comes on the scene. He sounds calm and jovial and full of authority. I get a good feeling which I can't explain, till I realize who it is. It is Huey McGooey.

I pull the chain and go back into the corridor. The girl has turned her back and leans against the wall, arms folded. Huey is pulling a string of flags from his sleeve. When he sees me, he beckons eagerly.

"Here's my friend Ben!"

The girl views me from the corner of her eye, wearily.

"Happy, Ben?" asks Huey.

"Great, thanks."

"Of course you are! You see, Becky? Everybody's happy but you!"

The girl turns back to the wall, with a sigh.

"Got everything you want?" Huey asks me.

"Yes thanks."

43

"Then I am happy too," says Huey, with a hand to his heart.

"Oh, there is one thing."

"Yes?" says Huey, slightly concerned.

"I want to go to the beach."

Huey nods thoughtfully. He puts an arm round my shoulder and guides me away from the girl and back into the Art Room. When he finally speaks he says nothing about the beach, and apologizes for the little scene with Becky, and asks me kindly not to mention it around the street. He seems so worried about it that I decide to leave aside my selfish concerns for the moment.

"What's the matter with her?" I ask.

"Sick, I'm afraid," says Huey.

"Is it catching?" I ask, nervously.

"Holy Moses, I should hope not!" says Huey. He taps his head. "In here, I mean."

"You mean she's a loony?"

Huey winces. "That's not a nice word, Ben," he says. "We prefer to say *paranoid schizophrenic*."

Huey notices I am clueless. He tells me he will explain as best he can. He sweeps an arm round the room.

"What do you see?" he asks.

"An art studio."

"Is it nice?"

"Brilliant."

"Now tell me, what are you painting?"

"Sunflowers."

"And are they beautiful?"

"Yeah."

"And what about these other good people? Are

they in a wonderful room, painting beautiful flowers?"

"Of course they are."

"And how do we know that?"

"Er…"

"We look at their paintings. Come along, Ben, let's do that."

Huey leads me round the circle of easels, an endless exhibition of pretty yellow sunflowers and strong green stalks and blue sky behind. The artists stand back as Huey passes and they exhange little pleasantries, the artists' heads bobbing gratefully as Huey speaks.

"Now," says Huey, in a graver voice, "we will see what Becky sees."

I am taken into a side-room, which is locked and bolted behind us. Huey takes a slow heave of breath and places his hand on a cupboard door.

"You don't have to go through with this, you know, Ben."

"It's all right."

"No, Ben. Whatever it is, it is not all right."

Huey opens the cupboard door. My heart drops to my boots. Inside the cupboard is a vision straight out of a thrashing nightmare. On a canvas five foot square is a vicious collision of blood-red, death-purple, acid-green and puke. Welded to the frame are a bubbling jungle of molten dolls' heads and splintered lockets and clockwork guts. And there, peering through the mess and the mutilation, with a corpse's eyes and blood-dripping hands, is the slashed, clawed and distorted face of Huey McGooey himself.

The real Huey McGooey closes the cupboard door

45

and for a moment casts his eyes to the floor. I feel a sudden urge to run to his defence, or to get that Becky for doing it, because it is just as if she has attacked him, not just the canvas.

"I'm sorry," says Huey. "But you did want to know."

"Why did she paint it?"

Huey shrugs. "She tells us it is what she sees."

There is a knock. Huey lets Stefan in. "She's gone," says Stefan. Huey nods.

"Can't you do anything for her?" I ask.

Huey sighs. "We've tried, Lord knows. We've given her chance after chance. We've even fixed her up with a doctor. A mind-doctor, you understand."

"All we want," says Stefan, "is that she should be happy."

"That's all we want for everybody," says Huey, and it seems to break the spell. He claps his hands. "Hey, come on! That's enough of the long faces! Life is short! There's fun to be had! Eurrgh, what's this in my pocket?"

Huey pulls out a trick plastic dog-turd. "Urgh! Urgh! Urgh!" he goes, jumping round the room, till I'm laughing my head off, and all the other artists are laughing too, even though they've no idea what I'm laughing about.

CHAPTER 5

Dear Mum + Dad
 Sorry I haven't had time
to write for a few days, but
there is so much to do I
hardly stop. I have met
Huey McGooey, he is great.
Tell Tracy I will get his
autograph when I remember.
 There is also a brilliant
beach here but I haven't
seen it yet.
 Love from Ben

Mr + Mrs Lewis
137 Goldacre
Milton Keynes
Bucks
 ENGLAND

Already, home seems a strange, foreign place. I'm
beginning to forget what people looked like. I've also
got used to not locking my door, and I hardly notice
as Alice and Hattie sail in, without even knocking.
They are dressed all in white, and covered in badges
saying *HEAT SEEKERS* and *I LOVE CLINT* and
ZAK FOR ME. They dive for my small collection of
singles, furiously throwing them this way and that.

"Careful!" I go.

"Don't worry," says Alice. "The staff'll clear it
up."

Hattie has been through all the records and looks
perplexed.

"Where are your Heat Seekers' records, Ben?"

"Who are the Heat Seekers?" I ask.

Their eyes open wide in astonishment.

"Everybody's heard of the Heat Seekers!" they
chorus together.

"I haven't."

"You *must* have! You *must* have!"

I decide I probably have heard of them after all and say that I thought they said *EAT SEAGULLS*. But I still haven't got any of their records. So Alice and Hattie immediately order me down to the floating megastore to buy their latest release.

Happy Street has its own radio station, its own TV, its own live music scene and its own charts. They are quite like normal charts except for two things. The first is that the records are all "holiday records". They do not say anything complicated or depressing, and the tunes and the rhythms are bouncy and breezy and suitable for all the family. The second is that the charts change every half-hour, instead of every week. This means that everyone can have the excitement of the top twenty countdown as often as they like, and have an endless supply of new sounds to spend their money on.

The floating megastore is run on exactly the same lines as any McGooey retail outlet. There are ten tills and no one waits more than two minutes. The records are served up exactly like the burgers, with a host of staff frantically pressing them in the Sound Kitchen behind. I unload a few Smiley Tokens, pocket my copy of "Bye Bye Baby Beach Love" by the Heat Seekers, then hurry back to the fun hut and proudly display it to Alice and Hattie. Hattie inspects the label with little interest, then puts the record aside and carries on fixing a Trouble Brothers badge to her stripy sweatshirt. I pick up the record and show her again.

"It's the Heat Seekers," I say. "The Heat Seekers, look."

Both of them look at me as if I am completely

stupid.

"Ben," says Alice, in a teacherly manner, "*no one* listens to the Heat Seekers any more."

Hattie takes pity. "Never mind, Ben," she says, "we'll take it to Radio Happy for the golden oldies programme."

Alice and Hattie also give me advice on my clothes. Fashion is much the same as the pop scene. New collections are announced several times a day. You can be the coolest person around at one end of Happy Street, and right out of date by the time you reach the other. Obviously it all costs a lot of money, but everyone's got money on Happy Street, and everyone loves spending it.

By the time evening comes round, I have bought three complete wardrobes of clothes and fifty-eight singles. Broken records are strewn all round my fun hut, after Alice and Hattie had a giggling fit and threw them against the wall. My bedside light is smashed as well, but Alice and Hattie say there are plenty more in Stores, and Mrs D will see to everything.

I put on my cape and baseball cap and set off for a good night's face-stuffing down the Cath, which is what cool people call the Burger Cathedral. This time I order a triple Brontoburger, fries, passion-fruit creamshake and double-cola with a helter-skelter straw. I wander out on to the patió, hoping to find DT and Tish, but I settle for a seat on my own, feet up on the wall, watching fireworks break over the forts. The sea is like glass tonight, and I can't imagine what that beach will look like, and despite what DT says, nothing interests me half as much.

Suddenly I duck down behind my double-cola. It's her, that girl again. She hasn't changed clothes since this morning. She moves between the tables with shoulders drooping and a miseryguts face, and I can't help it, but I wish the ground would open up and she would just drop into it. Other people make a deliberate attempt to face her with a big smile, by way of example to her, which she ignores.

She looks about for an empty seat and, oh God, she sees me. I get this terrible feeling, and the terrible feeling comes true. She heads straight towards me.

"This seat taken?" she says, then before I can answer, she says, "Cheers" and sits opposite me. She hangs one arm over the back of the chair, looks round and makes a face at somebody, then catches me watching.

"Yeah?" she says.

"Nothing."

She takes one of my chips, bites off an inch, then floppy-folds her arms on to the table, drops her chin on to them, and watches me.

"Been down the beach yet?" she asks.

"Not yet."

"Didn't think so."

"Why?"

She takes another chip, inspects it, and throws it over the edge towards the sea.

"Why what?" she says.

"Why didn't you think so?"

Becky is just about to answer when a group of babbling girls sit at the next table, all going on about Jimmy DuPont, the latest pop star. They argue passionately as to whether his favourite colour is magenta or violet. The argument grows louder till we have to turn away to hear ourselves speak.

"Why won't I get down the beach?" I ask again.

"They don't want you to, that's why."

"Why not?"

A group of lads have sat at the table the other side. They are arguing about whether it is possible to score a goal from an impossible angle. One says that football is a funny game and another says that what matters at the end of the day is how many you stick in the back of the net. The argument gets louder than the girls' conversation and I have this strange sensation that all the chairs are moving towards us and hemming us in. The closer they get and the louder they get, the more meaningless and trivial their arguments become, till my ears are full of nothing but sweeper systems and silly summer love.

Becky gives me a look of ancient tiredness, gets up, struggles through the crowd and out of the Cathedral.

Next day, Tish rings me and asks if I would like to spend the afternoon with her. She doesn't say where we are going, but something in her voice tells me it is going to be a big surprise. I pack my bathers and a towel, just in case.

We have arranged to meet at the Hanging Gardens of World Perfume. I find her choosing between Ucci D'amour and Yummo de Passion. She immediately offers both wrists to my nose and invites me to choose between them. I don't know anything about perfume, especially expensive perfume, so I say I like them both.

"Then I shall have them both," says Tish.

"Thank you, madam," says the sales lady. "That will be five thousand dollars."

Tish rummages through her handbag, but only has four-and-a-half thousand on her. She instructs the lady to charge it to her account. Then she asks me to take her arm, because she doesn't feel right without someone taking her arm.

I can see what she means. Seeing her without DT is like seeing the straight half of a comic act gone solo. She hangs quite tightly on to my skinny little arm, while I try to look cool, hindered only by the fact that my face has gone bright red.

We progress down Happy Street, with Tish holding her handbag before her like a little shield. I ask her where we are going.

"Why, shopping, of course," she says.

I try not to look disappointed.

Soon I am laden like a camel, with American football shirts and video games and the current best-selling album (Sal Monella's Greatest Hits, July – August). Tish won't let me pay for anything, even though I've got forty-nine thousand Smiley Tokens left in my wallet. I still haven't quite got round to confessing about those.

There is a fairground behind the Museum of Princesses, where Tish buys two Rio Grande choc-ices and tickets for the Big Wheel. She uses me as a support as she struggles into the seat on her towering high heels. I sit next to her, and off we go. The Big Wheel really is Big. It stops when we are at the highest point, giving us a panoramic view of the street, but not, unfortunately, of the beach. I show off by pointing out my fun hut and naming all the buildings. Well, almost all. There are two I don't recognize. One is a great red Victorian building, hidden behind the giant screens which show McGooey's latest world-wide adverts. The other is a long, low windowless white building, set back in the woods.

I ask Tish about the red building and the white building. She can't see the ones I'm on about. She suggests I ask DT, because he's on the Board, and he's sure to know. It quite worries Tish that I am so curious about everything. She says it's probably because I'm at the Awkward Age.

"Tell me, Ben," she says, suddenly turning to me, "do you have a girlfriend?"

This question, right out of the blue, totally floors me. I go all awkward, and she sees it and comes over all soft. That makes it even worse.

"Not at the moment," I blither.

Tish's head weaves from side to side, watching me closely, with a rather stupid smile on her face.

"And is that why you've been seeing Becky?" she asks.

Immediately I blurt out, "I'm not seeing her!" which is just about the worst thing I could have done. "Honest!" I add, and it sounds even worse.

"Ben," says Tish, "you've been seen with her."

"When?"

"I think you know when."

"Oh, *that*! I never asked her to sit next to me. I didn't want to talk to her."

Tish gives me a kindly ticking-off look. "You know about her problems, don't you?"

I don't know how Tish knows that I know about

53

Becky's problem. But I keep my lip buttoned. It's obviously the best thing.

"I know what you're thinking," says Tish.

"Do you?" I ask, warily.

"You think you can help her, don't you?"

"No, not really."

"You wouldn't be the first, Ben. But I'm afraid you're wasting your time. You see, I know it's sad, but some people are born like it. There is no other explanation. The ones you should feel sorry for are her mum and dad. They're lovely people, Ben. They've done nothing to deserve it. And she's said some terrible things about them. Horrible, horrible lies, about how they hate her, how they'd rather she was dead, how they've hit her, and I don't know what. What an awful thing, Ben, to set yourself against your own parents."

I nod politely. A surge of hope takes hold of Tish.

"You're such a nice young man, Ben. Here, I've got something for you."

Tish opens her handbag and takes out a flat parcel, about nine inches by six, wrapped in luxurious red silky paper. I reach for it but she holds it away.

"Now promise me you'll never talk to Becky again," she says.

"Yeah, yeah, sure."

Tish hands me the parcel. I work eagerly on the wrapping paper while she watches with expectant glee. As the last sheet comes away, she claps her hands together with childish excitement.

I find myself looking at a small painting of a beach.

"Well?" says Tish.

I've been given some useless presents in my time, and over the years I've got fairly expert at thinking up intelligent things to say about them. But this one really has got me beat.

"Is it … *the* beach?" I ask.

"Of course."

I suppose it is quite well painted. It's a very happy beach, with white Dovery cliffs and a big yellow sun and happy children playing at the water's edge.

"Stefan painted it," says Tish.

"Oh yeah. I thought I recognized the style."

"It is what you want, isn't it?"

"Yeah, sure."

"Say if it isn't. I can get it changed."

"No. It's great. Thanks very much."

"You know how you can thank me, don't you?" says Tish, softly.

"Stay away from Becky?"

Tish smiles victoriously, and squeezes my hand. "You're such a sensible young man," she says. "I'd so hate any harm to come to you."

CHAPTER 6

Tish's warning has exactly the opposite effect to what she intended. Previously I had no desire whatsoever to see Becky. Now she has become interesting, in a kind of unhealthy way, like it is interesting to put your finger in a flame. I start looking out for her. The trouble is, when I do see her, it's obvious that she is also looking out for me. Whenever she sees me, she makes a bee-line for me. I don't know what it is about me, but she's certainly latched on to me, and it's lucky I'm so good at dodging into the crowd and making a quick escape.

After a while I get to know her movements. I find safe hiding-places, where I can watch her, like watching some dangerous insect, half hoping it is suddenly going to strike out. At someone else, that is.

She's in a world of her own. Often she leans up against the wall, sketching idly with a stick of charcoal. People smile politely as they pass, and she scowls and asks them what they're looking at. Other times, she sits with her head between her knees, totally still, for hours on end. I remember pictures I've seen of old lunatic asylums, with staring-eyed freaks chained head and foot, sometimes for twenty years.

Once or twice, I find her in another mood. She stands hands in pockets, with a kind of eyebrows-up ah-well smile on her, chatting to one of the workers at the food stalls or swimming-pools. At these times I begin to wonder if she's got an identical twin.

Finally I make the mistake of creeping too close, trying to make sure it really is her. She sees me. There's no escape route. She comes straight for me. I panic. But just as it seems I will break my solemn promise to Tish, a crowd of pink track-suited joggers from the Health and Beauty Centre appear. Becky is caught up and whisked away, no more than two feet from reaching me.

I breathe again. Then I notice a biro lying at my feet. I pick it up. It is still warm, obviously from Becky's hand. There is no ink inside it. Instead, there is what looks to be a rolled piece of paper. I drop the biro into my pocket, checking that no one is watching. Then I hurry back to my hut, and tap out the paper on to a table. Just as I suspected, there is a message on it:

MEET ME TONIGHT
12 MIDNIGHT
PORCELAIN FOUNTAIN
BECKY.

I am truly terrified. I tear the paper into tiny pieces and flush them down the toilet. Then I pick up my pocket video game and try to forget all about it.

I am not sure at what point I decide to keep the appointment with Becky. In fact, I'm not sure I do make a conscious decision. It is more a growing feeling that it is inevitable. Every now and then I find myself glancing up at Stefan's picture, then checking my watch, then forgetting where I am in the video game. It is warm and cosy and safe in my fun hut, yet at a quarter to twelve, sure enough, I am lacing up my trainers.

I think again of the staring-eyed freaks. I remember other pictures, of lunatics being plunged into cold baths, and heads with peculiar dark eyes being wired up with electrodes. I remember stories of madwomen with superhuman strength. The words *paranoid schizophrenic* come back to me. I put a heavy snow-storm paperweight into my pocket, and hang a ref's whistle round my neck. Then I button up my jacket and walk into the night.

It is obvious why Becky has chosen the Porcelain Fountain. It stands in a quiet corner, at the opposite end of Happy Street to the Distant Star Stadium. The Distant Star is where the groups play, and everyone will be there tonight. It is a gi-normous arena where the performers can't actually be seen by most people, but that doesn't matter because the band's latest video will be shown on vast screens beside the stage. The videos are usually set in small sweaty clubs where you couldn't swing a cat. Last night Splat were playing, except they went out of date half way through, and were replaced by Split, while the toilets were jammed with people changing their T-shirts.

There is not one soul to watch over me as I approach the Porcelain Fountain. The fairy-lights of the fun huts are well behind me, there is silence, and the ghostly white fountain rears up in the moonlight. It is a fragile tower of china that weeps a thin milky water and looks like it wouldn't stand a breath of wind. Rumour has it that it was designed by a famous artist and meant for the Burger Cathedral, except the style was altogether wrong, and not at all Happy.

Because the artist was so famous, and McGooey's had spent so much money, they stuck it here and hoped no one would notice.

At first, Becky doesn't seem to be there. I feel almost relieved. Then something detaches itself from the base of the fountain and I realize she's been sitting there all along. She walks slowly towards me, while I walk slowly backwards.

"What's the matter?" she says.

"Nothing."

She stops. I stop. "It's this way," she says, with a nod of her head, a nod towards the dark rocky road the other side of the fountain.

"Why do you want to go?" I ask her.

"It's you that wants to go," she answers.

"What's in it for you?"

Becky folds her arms. "Nice quiet place, ain't it? No one'll hear your screams."

"Don't be stupid."

"Who's stupid?"

Pause.

"Not sure I want to go now," I mumble.

"Yes you do."

"How do you know?"

"I can see your hand shaking."

I stuff my hand back into my pocket.

"Come on," she says, and begins to walk.

I don't know why I follow. Perhaps it is because she is so decisive. She saunters along as if she walks this way every day, and maybe she does. I stay ten yards behind, watching for any false move, with my fingers sweaty on the paperweight. We reach a fork in the road, and Becky goes left, down a rough sandy

path. Along the path are lumps of tarmac and discard-
ed cats'-eyes, as if this was once a proper road. Now
it is a half-wilderness of ferns and bushes, with no
light except a half moon and stars.

We have gone maybe a hundred yards when two
figures appear up ahead. A torch-beam flashes.

"Looks like a fog coming in," says one.

"It does that. A right pea-souper," says the other.

The Laughing Police!

"Get down!" hisses Becky.

"It's only the —"

"Get down!" she hisses again, and we crouch
behind the ferns.

"What's this, Cowboys and Indians?" I sneer.

"Ssh!"

The Laughing Police amble past. Flossie is with
them. She gets a scent and rudders round towards us.

"What you got there," says the Admiral.

"She's smelled a rat," says the Bosun.

"Come on, girl," says the Admiral.

They wander on. Flossie abandons her trail and
scampers after them. I brush the ferns from my
clothes. "Bloody stupid," I mumble. Becky says nothing. I drop in line, ten yards behind again. I ask her
why she's so scared of the Laughing Police. I tell her
about the cup of cha I had with them. I tell her she
shouldn't be so prejudiced, just because they wear a
uniform. She doesn't say a thing.

Eventually we reach a chicken-wire fence, with
barbed wire running along the top. It cuts straight
across the sandy path, and right behind it is a sign:

BEWARE – SNAKE RESERVE.

Becky indicates a hole in the fence, just big enough to crawl through.

"Go on, then," she says.

"You're joking."

"What you scared of?"

"Can't you read?"

"That's bullshit. There's no snakes here."

"You go first then."

"All right."

Becky gets down on her stomach and wriggles through the hole. For a moment we stand on either side of the wire fence, as if I'm watching an animal in a cage, or as if I'm the animal, and she's watching me. There is a taunting look on her face.

"What a good little boy," she says. "Believes everything he's told."

She turns, ploughs off through knee-high bracken, the perfect habitat for adders and God-knows-what. I watch her till she has very nearly disappeared, then turn for home, then turn back and climb through the hole.

It is even darker on the other side of that fence. There are saplings blocking the moonlight, then thicker and thicker trees. I lean my weight on a branch, then snap it and twist it off. I swish the branch before me, and bang my feet down like a pantomime giant, because snakes are supposed to run away if they hear you coming. Becky takes no such precautions. She forges on through the bracken, while I slash and stab at tree roots and hanging ivy, or pulverize to death my own shadow.

The smell of the sea is growing stronger. I begin to walk faster, then trot, then run. The faster I run, the more the snake-panic takes hold of me. Finally I leap between two bushes and clatter right into Becky, who grabs my jacket. The stitches rip, and I jerk to a standstill. There is nothing in front of me. There is nothing but the soft rush of the sea, a long, long way below.

I remove Becky's hand from my jacket.

"Come on," she says.

Becky sets off down a steep flight of steps made of crumbling concrete. I take hold of a shaky wooden handrail and follow. The steps and the handrail disappear into the darkness below. Down I go, and down, and down. After a while I can no longer see the top, yet I still can't see the bottom, though the sea sounds a footstep away. I seize the handrail tightly, but it sways as if floating in space. I mutter my own name to myself, and my address, and the date, and what I am doing here. I lock my sights on the old flat cap going down before me. Down, and down, and down, until I am convinced I will never reach the bottom, at which point my feet sink into soft sand.

I'm there. I'm on the beach.

My first thought is to check the position of the steps, in case I need to make a getaway. This becomes easier when the moon slides out from behind the clouds. I realize I'm standing right next to a row of pedal-boats, nestling like piglets. I swing a leg over the nearest one, but my foot doesn't go down. The boat is full to the brim, with sand and seaweed and plastic bottles. They all are. The painted numbers on their sides are flaking away, and the oars lie broken or planted into the sand like hopeless trees.

Becky is clambering over some rocks and round a

headland. I walk slowly after, into the hard rippled sand near the water's edge, then across the crab pools and the slimy mounds of black seaweed. A new landscape opens up before me, a wide bay, but not an empty one. A curving line of beach huts runs round the back of it. There are exercise bars and a water-slide, an inflatable castle, a baby train, an ice-cream van, a bandstand. Deckchairs lie piled up in front of me. I open one, for a joke, but my hand goes through the canvas.

Becky has gone to the bandstand. I walk along in the shadow of the beach huts, feeling powerful, because I can see her but she can't see me. Most of the beach huts are roofless, with seagulls nesting. Windblown sand is piled against them, and over the wheels of the ice-cream van, and across the tracks of the baby train.

I kick at the sand, here and there, as if I could kick it all back where it came from. Then my toe cracks into something hard. It really hurts. I scrape furiously at the sand, ready to chuck it into the sea, whatever it is, to chuck it really, really hard so that it never comes back.

But it isn't a rock, or a shell, or anything from nature. It is a little head, on a pole. It grins up at me, a big cheesy grin, with a tormenting gleam in its eye. Its nose is long and hooked and so is the chin, and they almost meet, like pincers. The thing is caked with crude black oil, and teeming with mites and flies.

Punch. That's what it is. It's Punch.

"What's that?" says Becky, peering over.

I hold it up by the pole. She comes closer.

"Oh, God," she says. "Bury it."

Suddenly I push the Punch towards her face. "You're a naughty, naughty Judy!" I screech.

Becky jerks back. All of a sudden she seems very young, with her features flickering like a candle and tears welling up in her eyes.

"Don't!" she says.

I can't believe I was scared of her. I wave the Punch in her face again.

"You're a naughty, naughty — "

Becky swats the Punch from my hand. It drops into the sand, face up. She stamps it down, then kicks sand over it, then more sand. She buries it deep, then deeper still.

"What d'you do that for?" she snaps.

"It's only mucking about!"

"What d'you want to scare me for?"

"It's only a puppet, for Christ's sake!"

Becky storms off. I sink into a sulk, thinking what a typical girl she is, and how stupid I was, coming down with her. It's a crap beach. Even the deckchairs are rotten.

"See you then," I yell, and turn to go.

Becky doesn't answer. There is a metal box at the back of the bandstand, and she is working a piece of wire into the lock. Eventually she gets it open. The box is full of switches. Becky starts striking them down. Lights come on. She's turned on the flood-lights round the bandstand.

Lit by the brilliant white light, Becky walks out of the bandstand, half sits on the nearest floodlight, and yanks it round the other way. It flashes past my legs and on to the cliff behind. She does the same with the other floodlights. At first I pretend not to be interested in whatever she's doing, but after a while I can't resist a look behind me. And the moment I do, I get the biggest shock of my life.

The cliff is massive, and beautiful, every colour under the sun. But there is something very wrong with it. Rather than rising straight from the beach, it curves over us, miles over us, almost as if the beach is inside a giant cave. The buildings of Happy Street must be right above us and that glow at the very edge must be the patio of the Burger Cathedral. Yet there is nothing beneath it all! Nothing but a few feet of sandstone, then a yawning gap, a breathless drop, and the sea waiting.

A page of my geog book springs to mind. It is a diagram of an eroded cliff. The sea has eaten away at the bottom of the cliff. Eventually, the cliff will be eaten back so far that the top collapses and the whole lot crumbles. Now that little black-and-white drawing has come to terrifying, full-colour life.

For a moment I wonder if there is something wrong with my eyes. I turn to Becky, who is watching me coolly, arms folded.

"Jesus," I say.

"He won't help," says Becky.

"What's holding it up?"

Becky shrugs.

"That sea must be vicious!" I say.

"Who says the sea did it?" says Becky.

"What else could do *that*?"

Becky takes a long breath. "Remember the path we came down?" she says. "Used to be a road, didn't it?"

"So?"

"Well, once upon a time, not so very long ago, that road was full of little men, in little red McGooey's trucks. And you know what they were carrying?"

"What?"

"Bricks. Big bricks. To build their big buildings out of. And do you know where they got them from?"

I swing round to the cliff, open-mouthed, then back to Becky.

"They wouldn't be that stupid!"

Becky starts to jig, from side to side.

"Hu–ey McGooey … is the funniest clown!

See … him drop … his trousers down!"

"They wouldn't be that stupid!" I repeat, but she just carries on: "With his nose so red … and his bur-gers so chewy!"

I start marching around the beach, first in one direction, then another.

"We've got to do something!" I yell.

"The *funn–i–est* clown … is – "

"Shut up! We've got to do something!"

"Hu–ey … McGooey!"

Becky finishes by throwing out both her arms, which then drop limply to her sides. "Go on, then," she says.

I stare at her, in disbelief. She does a silly smile.

"You *are* mad," I go.

"Course I am," says Becky. "We all are."

"*I'm* not!"

"Not yet," says Becky.

CHAPTER 7

Next morning the sun is shining, the birds twitter, fun buggies run busily this way and that, and groups chat lazily about the morning news. It is like every other morning on Happy Street, except my hands are clamped to the wall of the Circular Screen Cinema, feeling my way slowly along, terrified of every crack in the paving stones.

"Morning, Ben!" says the Video-Mart manager, strolling by. "Morning, Ben!" says the Water Fun Park attendant. They all assume I am on one of the Fame School's outdoor drama workshops. But I am on a mission to find DT, a mission to prevent the unthinkable disaster that faces all of us.

Alice and Hattie are at the badges stall. I call to them.

"Where's your dad?"

They run over. I wince at their clumping feet.

"Ben!" says Alice. "Have you got any Heat Seekers records?"

"They're back in," says Hattie. "There's a nostalgia boom."

"Sod the Heat Seekers, where's your dad?"

Alice and Hattie go open-mouthed to each other.

"Ben swore!"

I take one hand off the wall and wave it in their faces.

"Listen! This is important!"

"Not more important than the Heat Seekers," says Alice.

"Are you all right, Ben?" says Hattie.

"Yes. I'm all right. I just want to see your dad. Look, you can have all my Heat Seekers records if you just tell us where he is."

They immediately decide it's a deal.

"Top floor, Dallas Fantasy," says Hattie.

"Cheers," I go, pawing away down the wall, to their cries of "Where're the records?"

The Dallas Fantasy is the tallest building on Happy Street. It is a giant prong of blue sandstone poking into the sky, supporting sheets of black mirror glass which speak of mystery and power, and more pocket money than you could ever dream of. The Dallas Fantasy has the strange effect of making you feel part of something great, while at the same time being very, very tiny.

In the entrance hall are full-grown oak trees, and a massive pair of ornamental bull's horns suspended over bronze letters the size of statues reading McGOOEY INTERNATIONAL. Men in blue suits stroll about everywhere with portaphones on each shoulder, saying "It's a deal" or "Buy him out" or "Don't expect me home, dear". The ones with identity photos are on the Board. Some say that the Board own Happy Street. Others say they merely run it. I have also heard that they neither own it nor run it, just play at owning and running it. It is true that there is a corridor connecting the Dallas Fantasy with the Fame School. But whatever the Board really does is a mystery to everybody except the Board.

I take the glass bubble that runs up the centre of the building, surrounded by a tropical aquarium filled with bizarre fish and the occasional scuba-diver. On the top floor I find DT's harem. DT's harem is only called a harem for a joke (I think). There are seven secretaries, recruited from fashion shows and under-arm deodorant ads. They all say "Ah!" and try to mother me, but when I get serious they become very snappy and tell me what a busy and important man DT is. I ignore their protests and show myself straight into his office.

DT's office is the size of a tennis court. Far away by the window is an antique desk and behind that is DT himself, swivelling gently. A pungent smell of leather and expensive after-shave comes to my nostrils.

"Ben!" says DT. "This *is* an unexpected pleasure!"

I set off towards him and immediately sink to my ankles in the lush Persian carpet. At the end of my long trek I find DT holding a small gadget between finger and thumb.

"Darn little thing," he says. "Know what that is, Ben?"

He hands me the gadget, which looks like a miniature mileometer.

"It's an air-meter, Ben. Clips on the nose. See?"

DT takes the gadget and clips it on to his nose.

"Boys downstairs came up with it this morning," he says, nasally.

I nod briefly and try to deliver my urgent message, but DT has not finished his own.

"We're in everything, Ben. Fast food, leisure, oil, coal, entertainments, fashion, drinking water, you name it. Just one thing we're not in, Ben, and that's air. Damn stuff's given away free. Any fool can take a sniff on it. But this little fellow here, this could change all that."

DT unclips the gadget and lays it reverently on the desk between us.

"Got to come, Ben. If we don't get there, someone else will."

DT sits back, well satisfied, and selects a cigar from his top drawer. At this point he notices I'm shaking.

"Say, is anything the matter?" he asks.

"Yes," I peep.

A look of grave concern and urgency comes over DT. He presses his intercom and tells Laura to hold all his calls. He snaps open his lighter and tells me to fire away.

"I've been to the beach," I blurt.

DT's fingers freeze on the lighter. "You've been to the beach?"

"Last night."

"Well," says DT, "you *are* an enterprising fellow." He lights his cigar, and slow-blows the smoke.

"I saw something. Something serious."

"Go on."

"There's nothing beneath Happy Street."

DT sits forward. "Nothing beneath Happy Street?"

"They've cut into the cliff. That's what the street's built out of. The cliff. We're just hanging over the air."

DT stands. He paces slowly across the room, and gives the wall a good punch. "Feels solid enough to me," he says.

"I'm not making it up," I tell him.

DT paces slowly behind me, and lays a fatherly

hand on my shoulder.

"I'm sure you're not, Ben," he says.

"What are you going to do?"

"Well ... there's a Board meeting on Tuesday..."

"We've got to get everyone out now!" I go, trying to jump up, but held down by DT's strong hands.

"Ben," he says, firmly. "You're almost a man. Now control yourself."

I stop resisting, and sink back down. DT comes round and sits on the edge of the desk, waiting for my breathing to slow.

"And how does a man deal with a problem like this?" he asks, quietly, like a kindly teacher.

I shake my head.

"*Systematically* and *methodically*," says DT and the very words seem to shore up the teetering cliff.

I tell him I was just about to say that.

"You must understand, Ben. Happy Street is not the corner shop. Happy Street represents many millions of dollars to McGooey's. One hint of bad news and the shares will be tumbling. The whole enterprise will collapse like a pack of cards. That's why we don't run around screaming and panicking. If we've got a problem, we've got the best boys in the world to deal with it. Engineers, geologists, you name it. Now I'll tell you what I'll do for you, Ben. I'll call an extraordinary general meeting of the Board this very afternoon. I shall label the matter High Priority. How will that suit you?"

"Thank you."

"Now you get back to your hut and sit tight, and we'll get someone round to see you."

"Thank you."

"And in the meantime, not a word to anyone. Understood?"

"Yes."

"You're growing up fast, Ben."

DT gives me a farewell handshake, and I make my way back through the carpet, feeling so much better, as if I've had a warm mug of Ovaltine and bedtime story rolled into one.

"Thank you," I repeat, yet again, as I open the door.

"Oh, and Ben…" says DT.

"Yes?"

"Keep smiling, eh?"

No more than an hour after my visit to DT, there is a knock at my door. I open it to find a man of about thirty, in a green cord jacket, with a gingery fringe which tickles his trendy specs.

"Hello, Ben," he says, as if we are old friends.

"Hello?"

"May I come in?"

"If you like."

"Thanks, Ben. Thanks a lot."

The strange man ambles in, rubbing his hands together nervously. His eyes scan quickly round my games and posters and thrown-down clothes. He says what a nice room I have, which is odd, because all the fun huts are exactly the same.

"May I…?" he says, and takes a seat anyway. I stand awkwardly, but he suggests that I sit back on the bed and make myself comfortable, as it may be a long interview. There is something sympathetic in his tone, as if I am recovering from some kind of accident. I settle back, self-consciously. He takes out a notepad.

"Let's hear about it," he says.

"About what?"

"Your problem."

"You mean the cliff?"

"Exactly."

"That's not my problem. That's everyone's."

"As you wish. Carry on."

"It's going to collapse."

"I see. Why is that, Ben?"

"Because they've used it all for bricks."

"They?"

"McGooey's."

The strange man taps his teeth with his pen. "And when was this?" he asks.

"I don't know. When they built the street, I suppose."

"Oh," says the strange man. "I was under the impression that you *saw* this happen."

"No, I never saw it, no."

The man makes a little note. "So you are simply repeating what someone else has told you?"

"No!" I say, then on second thoughts, "Yes."

The strange man makes several more notes, each one draining a drop more confidence from me.

"I did see the cliff," I tell him, but he doesn't respond, at least he doesn't seem to. But when he has finished writing, he takes a long hard look at me, and says, "I know."

"You mean you believe me?"

The strange man holds up a hand. "Ah," he says. "Now that's another matter."

"I wouldn't have made it up!"

"No, Ben, I'm sure you wouldn't. Have a look at this, would you?"

The man hands me a sheet of paper, on which is the following diagram:

"What do you see?" he asks.

"A vase."

"Not two faces, looking at each other?"

I look again. "Oh yeah."

"But you just said it was a vase."

"It is. It's either."

The man folds and pockets the paper. "The brain," he says, "is a highly complex organ. We are still only beginning to understand how it works."

"There's nothing wrong with my brain."

The man stops. "What an odd thing to say," he says.

"I thought you were saying there was something

74

wrong with me."

This time the man makes no reply, just a note on his pad.

"As I was saying," he continues, "the brain is not as straightforward as we once imagined. We are not computers. Think of all those people, Ben, lost in the desert, desperate for water, and those incredible visions they have seen, of green trees and pools of fresh clean water. Think of those nuns in their hair shirts, half starved, suddenly seeing the radiant face of the Virgin Mary on the convent wall. They all have one thing in common, Ben. They see ... what they *want* to see."

I think on this. "Why should I want to see a hole in the cliff?" I ask him.

"That," says the strange man, "is what I am here to find out."

He smiles. I sit up. "Who are you, anyway?" I ask him.

"Never mind about me," he says.

"Are you a mind-doctor?" I ask, with growing fear.

"Never mind about me," he repeats.

"There's nothing wrong with me!" I say, but even as I say it, I get a sudden vision of myself as dangerous and unstable.

"Ben," says the mind-doctor, firmly, "the first step towards a cure is to face up to your condition. These hallucinations are a part of that condition."

"What condition?"

The mind-doctor raises both hands. "Let's keep our head on, shall we?" he says.

The mind-doctor turns another page of his notepad. "I'm going to give you a few words," he says, "and I want you to give me the first word that comes into your head. OK?"

The mind-doctor raises his eyebrows and smiles. I stare back stonily.

"Tree," he says.

I don't answer. He waits. "Timber," I grunt.

"Snake."

"Venom."

"Snow."

"Avalanche."

"Nail."

"Coffin."

"Water."

"Drown."

"Sunflower."

"Weedkiller."

"Tell me, Ben," he says, tapping his pen sharply on the pad, "how long have you been fascinated by death?"

"Since last night."

The mind-doctor scribbles busily, then rips a page from his notepad and holds it in his hand.

"Exactly what I'd expect," he says. "For a person with your condition."

"What condition?"

"Very well. If you really must know, you have all the classic symptoms of … *paranoid schizophrenia*."

The words strike like a deadly curse. I sit in total stupor as the mind-doctor babbles on about the pre-scription he has written, and tells me I can pick it up from the Doctor Druggo Superstore. He pushes the piece of paper into my hand, and I gaze at it as if Blind Pew has given me the Black Spot.

"We're all on your side, Ben," says the mind-doctor, and his face shows a concern which can only be genuine.

CHAPTER 8

I refuse to believe that DT sent the mind-doctor. I'd like to think he didn't even know about it. Someone else on the Board must have it in for me. Perhaps their son or daughter entered the poetry competition and got second prize.

Anyway, they will soon be sorry. I am writing a letter to Huey McGooey. The letter goes like this.

Honolulu Fun Hut
Happy Street

Dear Mr McGooey,

I am sorry to say I have a complaint about my holiday in Happy Street. Last night I went down to the beach and I think you ought to know the cliff is dangerous because all the rock has been taken away and soon everything will cave in and we will all be killed. I told D.T. all about this and he said he would tell the Board, but all that happened was that the mind-doctor came to visit me and said I was seeing things and had mental problems. I am not seeing things, I am telling the truth, and I know you'll believe me and do something about it quickly.

I just thought you ought to know what is going on in your street.

Yours sincerely,
Ben Lewis

I mail the letter on the McGooey Pigeon Post, which goes twelve times a day and is the fastest in the world. That same evening I get the following reply:

The Happy Palace
Happy Street

Dear Ben,

Many thanks for your letter, which I passed on to Mr McGooey this afternoon.

Mr McGooey asked me to make the following comments:

Mr McGooey enjoyed your story immensely. The handwriting was neat and clear and the spelling excellent. The story shows great imagination and a good eye for detail. Mr McGooey particularly liked the passage about the cliff, and thought the scene with the "mind-doctor" was quite hilarious. Mr McGooey likes a nice twist in the end of a story, and you are obviously very good at them.

However, Mr McGooey felt that, overall, the story was not quite up to the standard of your poem, and he is sorry to say he will not be able to use it for his next advert. He suggests you try adding a happy ending. Perhaps you and Mr McGooey could arrive in the Happycopter and save Happy Street by dropping a huge load of chicken nuggets on to the beach.

I hope you will not find this reply too disappointing.

Yours smilingly,

Antony Fishbone-Riley

Antony Fishbone-Riley

Secretary to Mr Huey McGooey

I read this letter once, twice, and finally three times. The words do not change. At this point I reach a momentous decision: I am going home. With a fumbling finger I stab out the number of the operator.

"Happy Telecom!" she says, brightly. "Can I help you?"

"I want to ring my mum," I blub.

"Certainly, sir. Have you her happyphone number?"

"She hasn't got a happyphone number. It's Milton Keynes 862551."

"I'm awfully sorry, sir. Happy Telecom has no contact with the outside world."

"Why not?"

"It is our policy, sir, not to allow unhappiness down the phone lines."

"That's stupid!"

"Our aim is to protect you, sir, and the unique holiday atmosphere of Happy Street."

The operator sounds just like one of those pre-recorded talking dolls. There is little point in arguing.

"Get me the train station."

"Certainly, sir."

There is a buzz, a click, a ding-dong, and finally a jovial voice.

"Happy Street Halt! Can I help you?"

"When's the next train?"

"The next train where, sir?"

"The next train out."

"Won't keep you a moment, sir."

I scrabble for a well-bitten pencil and scrap of paper.

"Here we are, sir. Ten forty-two, sir."

I scribble it down.

"On the twenty-fifth of August, sir."

My pencil drops. "What? That's ... nearly two weeks!"

"That's correct, sir. We don't run as many as we used to. Must make a profit you see, sir. Keep everybody happy."

I replace the phone in the middle of his cheerful farewell. An awful feeling has come over me, a feeling that the walls of my fun hut are slowly but surely moving in towards me.

Once I was doing a quiz with Jonno. He asked who won the FA Cup in 1964, and I said, "West Ham." "Wrong," said Jonno. "Who was it then?" I asked him. "West Ham," he said. "I just *said* West Ham!" I said. "You said West Brom," he said. "You deaf idiot, I said West Ham!" I said. And he said I never, and I *swore* I did. Only, unknown to me, he'd had his tape recorder on all the time. He wound it back. And there on the tape, as clear as you like, was my voice saying "West Brom".

Can I really have made a mistake about the cliff? The more hours that pass, the less sure I am. The mind-doctor seemed *so* certain of himself. And if he's right, and I never saw what I thought I saw, could it be there really *is* something wrong with me?

There is only one way to know. I have got to go in search of the cause of all my problems. Becky.

I find Becky chatting to a street cleaner, in one of her better moods, with hands in pockets and the ah-well

81

smile. That smile quickly fades as she catches sight of me, crouched close to the ground and clinging to the wall of the Happy Ending Bookshop.

She leaves the cleaner and comes over to me.

"Want a cup of tea?" she says.

"They've sent the mind-doctor to see me," I tell her, grimly.

"Nice experience, eh?" she says, cheerily.

"It's not funny."

"Come on then, if you want to talk about it."

Becky strolls down the little arcade by the bookshop, past the olde-worlde gas lights, towards the West Side fun huts. I scramble like Quasimodo after her. She sorts out a key and makes her way into one of the huts.

Somehow, Becky's hut seems half the size, and twice the darkness, of any other hut on Happy Street. The windows are pasted up with polythene and cardboard. The walls are a dirty funeral purple. The furniture has been replaced by a scabby old kitchen cabinet, painted acid green. Anything which might make the place seem homely has been torn up or taken out. The cushions have gone from the chair. The mattress has gone from the bed. On the floor is a tatty sleeping-bag, and various squares of wood, covered in explosions of oil-pastel. On the shelves there are a stack of secondhand, yellowy paperbacks, and a dozen empty bottles of Happy Juice, some with candle-stumps, some with an inch of juice left, carpeted in mould.

"Make yourself at home," says Becky, boiling an old camping-kettle.

I settle awkwardly in the chair, next to an old-fashioned record player with an LP of Leonard Cohen still spinning. Becky presents me with a half-pint tin mug of tea, and sits opposite me, with a block of computer paper and a stick of charcoal. She steers the charcoal over the paper with great determination.

"I saw that cliff," I say. "Didn't I?"

"You tell me," says Becky.

"Don't muck about! That mind-doctor's already got me doubting."

"Oh, he's good at that," says Becky.

"It *was* real, wasn't it?"

"You saw it."

"But no one believes me! I told DT, and I could tell he didn't. Now I'm scared to open my mouth."

Becky finishes her charcoal line and views her picture from a few different angles. "God, you're innocent," she says.

"Why?"

"Course they believe it. Why d'you think they didn't want you to go down there?"

"Then why don't they *do* something?"

Becky makes no reply. Her spare hand dabs about the floor, finds its way round a bottle of Happy Juice, and lifts it to her mouth.

I bang my mug down hard. "Why did you take me down there?"

Becky finishes her swig and wipes her mouth with her sleeve. "You wanted to go."

"But you *knew* what would happen!"

There is just the tiniest flicker of guilt over Becky's face, then it hardens. "Got to grow up sometime," she says, and starts whipping lines of charcoal across her drawing.

"Well, I'm not scared of them," I say, rocking angrily in the chair. "I'm going to get a knife, and get someone hostage, and – "

At this moment, I tip back too far, the chair overbalances, and my arms and legs go everywhere. Becky leaps to her feet and pulls me back just before my head can crack against the wall.

"Are you all right?" she says.

"Yeah," I go, heart banging.

"Should be more careful," she says, pulling her scratty carpet under the back legs of the chair.

I have not seen Alice and Hattie since I promised them my Heat Seekers records. To be honest, I don't expect to see them, after the way I spoke to them. Yet hardly have I arrived back at my hut when there they are, breezing in, as cheerful as you like.

"We've got you a ticket," says Alice.

"We thought it might cheer you up," says Hattie.

"Who says I need cheering up?"

Hattie's eyes flash quickly from side to side. "You know, I can't remember," she says.

"Word gets round, you know," gabbles Alice. "Especially if someone's unhappy."

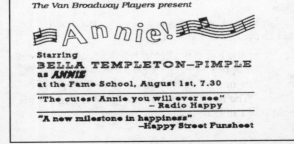

I look at the ticket they have handed me.

My first thought is that all those people in one building, cheering and clapping, might just be enough to bring about the final collapse. Then it occurs to me that this is my golden opportunity to announce to everybody the danger we are in. The thought of getting up on stage is almost as frightening to me as the prospect of falling to a horrible death. But I know it must be done.

I have never been to the theatre, but I have seen the Royal Variety Performance on TV, and the scene at the Fame School is very similar. Huey McGooey arrives in a black fun buggy, and is introduced to the cast, who bow and curtsy and make nervous polite replies to his calm polite questions. The foyer is full of dinner jackets and gowns, and it's Darling this and Darling that, and strange faces peering into mine and asking me if I wasn't Macavity in *Cats*. I crouch with one arm round a pillar, as if that could save me, and picture them all, drowned and mangled and buried alive. I hear the ear-piercing screams as the ground opens up like a giant throat, and the ball gowns and dinner jackets suddenly find nothing beneath them but thin air and death. I edge into my seat, head down, muttering frantically the speech I have prepared. The lights go down, and the blood thumps round my temples like a bass drum.

There is a round of applause. The curtain is up and Bella has appeared, with an imitation shaggy dog and a red bow in her hair. She presses her finger into her dimple. The applause doubles. I grip the arms of my seat as if I'm in a plummeting airliner.

Alice is shaking my arm. "Are you all right, Ben?"

"Too much excitement," I mumble.

"You can never have too much excitement!" says Hattie, clapping her hands in glee.

Redgrave and Oliver do a silly cockney dance routine, then Bella does a sad little song to her shaggy dog, which has everybody snuffling into their hankies. Soon they are laughing again, till the stage lights rattle, and I mumble "Shut up! Shut up, everyone, it's not funny!"

At the finale, the whole crowd rises as one, whistling, cheering, stamping and waving their programmes. Lottie van Broadway emerges from behind her piano, and holds out her hand for the entire cast to come skipping back on. Their show has finished, mine has just begun.

I begin my long lonely walk down the aisle, staggering from one row of chairs to the next, as if I am a drunk working my way down a speeding train. Lottie van Broadway spots me and turns with open arms as I clamber on to the stage. She is obviously expecting flowers. When she realizes I'm trying to say something, she assumes I must be making a speech of congratulations, and hushes the audience for me. There is a rumour that the Happy Street Oscars may be presented tonight, and the cast clasp their hands together like backstage at Miss World. Everything goes very quiet.

"Ladies and gentlemen!" I begin.

I peer out to see them all, heads on one side, polite expressions, as if I am something delightful. I look straight at Huey. He seems a little puzzled.

"I have ... a very important announcement!"

A whisper goes along the cast: "Bella's got it."

"Bella's got the Oscar." Bella takes a piece of paper out of her pocket and gives it a quick glance, lips mumbling.

"The ground beneath us," I pronounce, "is about to give way!"

Everybody immediately looks down.

"We must do something quickly," I continue, "or we will all die!"

Lottie Van Broadway's smile drops. Bella puts the paper back in her pocket. Someone whispers "Is this part of the play?" Others take it up: "It's part of the play!" There is laughter.

"It's not a joke!" I yell. "It's not a joke, and it's not part of the play! Just go down to the beach, you'll see what I'm on about!"

There is confusion, and the beginnings of consternation. You can feel it spread through the crowd, like a sea-wave. Suddenly a large woman in a silver fox-fur gets to her feet and points directly at me.

"I do not know who you are," she says, "but I suggest you get down off that stage this minute. For the past hour I have watched a cast of marvellous, talented children on that stage and I *cannot* understand why anybody should want to ruin *their moment*. I suggest you are a jealous, silly little boy and I for one am not going to have my evening ruined by this infantile … prank! Thank you, Miss Van Broadway, for one of the best nights of my life!"

She sits, with a determined thump, to a great round of applause. Someone boos me. Others take it up. I feel like I'm drowning. Huey sits very still, smiling his inevitable painted smile. The booing gets louder, and with it comes the whistling, the jeering, the shouts of "Get off!"

Lottie Van Broadway turns to me, with a bitter little smile.

"Isn't that a *horrible* sound, Ben?" she says.

CHAPTER 9

Happy Street has become the street of shame. I have never been so humilated, not even when the school football team was called up on stage because someone had soiled their shorts. I don't want to speak to anyone and I don't want anyone to speak to me. For the next day I stay locked in my fun hut, listening to the voices outside the door, convinced they are talking about me. I try turning on the radio, but the good-time summer songs have become strangely sinister, and the waffling DJ is yet another part of the plot against me.

Eventually, however, I know I've got to eat, and that means stepping outside the door. By tea-time, the hunger pangs have become too much to bear. I pull my collar up over my face and slope off outside, in the shadows.

"Afternoon, Ben!" says Mr Braddock, my neighbour.

Obviously he wasn't at the Fame School last night.

"Afternoon, Ben!" says Colin, the fun buggy mechanic.

This is harder to explain. I'm sure I saw him in the foyer.

"Afternoon, Ben!" says Pat, the pigeon post-woman.

"How are you going?" says Jem, from over the road.

By now I am becoming suspicious. They can't all have missed *Annie*. Nor can all those other smiling

89

faces. It is becoming obvious that every person I meet will be just as friendly today as they were yesterday. It is uncanny.

Just beyond the Fanti Cola Arch comes the acid test. The fox-fur woman is walking directly towards me. I cringe as I remember the tongue-lashing she gave me less than twenty-four hours ago.

We come face to face. "*Good* afternoon, Ben," she says, warmly.

The fox-fur woman passes on, with a joyful swagger. My amazed eyes follow her past the Water-fun pool, where I catch sight of Alice and Hattie playing with a large beach ball. They wave enthusiastically. I am too stunned to realize that I am waving limply back.

Alice and Hattie abandon their beach ball and skip over. They offer me a ticket to the Underdogs concert tonight.

"I'm not going out any more," I tell them.

"Why not?" says Alice.

"Obvious, isn't it?"

Not to Alice and Hattie.

"Well, Ben," says Hattie, "if you don't want to go, you don't have to go."

They turn away. I reach forward and put a hand on Alice's shoulder. She looks down on it as if she's grown another head.

"Why are you being so nice?" I ask them.

"What do you mean?" says Alice.

"Everyone's being nice. Why are you being so nice?"

"How would you like us to be, Ben?" says Hattie, coyly.

"I don't know! Normal!"

Alice and Hattie are equally baffled.

"But we are normal, Ben," says Alice.

Alice turns to the crowd on her left, then the crowd on her right. Nothing but happy-dolly faces, happy-dolly faces, all slightly self-conscious, as if their photos are being taken.

"It's not a crime to be happy," says Hattie, primly.

"What about unhappy?"

"Unhappy?"

"Is it a crime to be unhappy?"

I seem to be speaking a foreign language.

"It's like last night never happened!" I go.

"Last night?" says Alice.

"What, the play?" says Hattie.

"My speech!"

"What speech?"

"About the cliff!"

"What cliff?"

Suddenly all the tension and frustration of the last two days boils up in me. "What are you anyway?" I yell. "Robots?" Next second my hands are at Alice's throat, twisting at her head, as if I could twist it off and find the wires beneath. I hear her gasp, but all control has gone. I feel Hattie pulling frantically on my arm, and the crowd rushing in. "Ben!" I hear. "Ben, what are you doing?"

My hands come away. I raise them, like a footballer who's just hacked down the opposition. I can still feel the sensation of that thin, warm, fragile throat.

The crowd parts, and a familiar figure pushes through.

Holiday in Happy Street

"I'm sorry, Ben," says the mind-doctor, "but we're going to have to take you to the Happy House."

CHAPTER 10

It has just turned dark as we reach the McGooey International Happy House Institute. As if it was a dream, I remember my trip on the Big Wheel, and the mysterious red building. Now I am being marched into that same building, with my arms trapped against my body by a straitjacket. Through the frosted windows come horrible moanings, and screams, and shadows looming twenty foot tall. I struggle again, but each time I struggle it makes me madder and madder, as if an iron band is being tightened around my head. I know I have been yelling and screaming for the past half hour, but about what, I do not know.

The mind-doctor's assistants hustle me through the doors and into an entrance lobby which smells of old wood and antiseptic. An old lady in her dressing gown is clinging to the radiator, babbling. She gives me a cracked, vacant smile. I am hurried on, down a long white corridor, spotlessly clean, past mysterious doors which say ELECTRO-CONVULSIVE THERAPY, and CLINICAL RESEARCH and OPERATING THEATRE. Signs at the end of the corridor read BLACK SECTION – FEMALE, and WHITE SECTION – MALE. It is obviously an enormous institution.

Finally, I am guided into the mind-doctor's office, and sat before his desk. My possessions are placed before him, including my entire collection of Smiley Tokens, and the keyring my sister gave me, and my best hankie. I sit zombie-like under the bright light, while he pokes through them with his finger, then signs a form handed him by an assistant.

A tear wells up in my eye and rolls down my cheek. The assistants look to the mind-doctor as if they should do something about this.

"It's all right, Jimmy," says the mind-doctor. "Strong emotions are one of the typical features of these cases."

The tears are followed by a line of snot which I cannot prevent escaping from my nose. I sit there with it stuck to my face, feeling it hardly matters.

"OK, boys," says the mind-doctor. "Let's have him out of there."

The assistants unfasten and remove my straitjacket. I shake my arms limply. They are bruised and aching.

The mind-doctor hands me my own hankie and asks me to wipe my nose.

"I'm supposed to be on holiday," I whimper.

"Ben," says the mind-doctor, "you are not the only person on Happy Street. We have the safety of five thousand others to consider."

"Let me go home then."

"You shall go home, Ben. As soon as you are cured. We're going to put you on South Pacific ward. You'll have a programme of cold showers, counselling and work therapy. If you make progress, we will not have to resort to more, er, extreme measures. Is that understood?"

He asks me this as if I am about five. Then he instructs the assistants to take me off for my first shower and an early night to follow.

I shower in a large china sink in the centre of a

massive decaying washroom, surrounded by about two hundred doorless toilets, and watched over by the assistants. The water is freezing, and I am frail and white and shivering, like a small frightened animal. The assistants watch with that same sense of power and satisfaction as Mr Morris, when he stands with his hand on the temperature control after Games. I am handed a clean white uniform of hard cotton, and led down the ward.

By now, lights have gone out in the wards, but the sounds carry on just the same. I am taken past row after row of bunk beds, where unknown voices groan and mumble "No!" and talk in machine-gun bursts to imaginary audiences. Most are lying in their beds, but we come across two men, squatting in the middle of the floor, hugging each other. Another is sitting bolt upright in his bed, with an astonished stare, and hair that seems to stand on end. Into the middle of this circus of freaks I am guided to my bunk. It is a bottom bunk, with a thin army blanket and starched sheets tugged tight across. They leave me to crawl inside. I watch the hunched figures on either side, babbling through their private hells, and I imagine myself anywhere else but here.

Suddenly a hand drops down from a bunk above. It is skinny, and old, with liver patches and a forest of grey hair. I lie absolutely still. The hand whisks the air. It moves towards me. Before I have a chance to jump back, it is on my face, running across it like a strong bony spider, finally clamping on my chin, and stroking hard down the side of it.

"Ah," says a voice from above. "A young 'un."

Next second there is a face beside me, upside-

down, grinning toothlessly. I shrink back in horror.
For over a week I have not seen an ugly face. I had
forgotten just how ugly a face could be. It looks as if
it has been boiled for a week. One eye is dead and
turned aside. The other has that strange blackness
around it. The nose is broken and pushed almost flat.
The gaping toothless mouth is hooked in the centre
like a parrot's beak.

"What you in for?" it says.

"Paranoid schizophrenia," I blurt.

"Ah," it says, "senile dementia, me. Got a fag?"

"Don't smoke."

"They tried to take my lighter. But I hid it. Look."

The man shows me a small disposable lighter, and
cackles.

"You can call me Grandad," he says.

"I'm Ben," I tell him.

"Pleased to meet you, Ben."

"And by the way, there's nothing wrong with me."

Grandad's only reply is "Ha!" There seems little
point in telling him the story about the cliff, but I tell
it anyway, if only to convince myself.

Grandad takes little interest in the story, and much
more in my hair, which he handles with curious fascination, like babies do. I inch myself away and tell
him that he might as well know that the cliff will fall
and we will all die.

"Oh, aye," says Grandad.

"Listen," I say to him. "I am not mad. The cliff …
is going … to fall."

"Oh, aye. Aye, I know that."

I look into his one eye. "You know that?"

"Oh, aye. Course I do. We all do. That is why

we're here."

Without another word, Grandad slides back up into his bunk, and soon is snoring peacefully.

Everything looks very different, knowing I am not alone. I lie awake in that horrible ward, feeling a strange excitement and unexpected hope. I listen closely to the ranting and babbling, and some of it begins to make sense. But whenever I whisper across the ward, trying to make contact, everything goes quiet, as if I'm disturbing a well-worn routine.

I hardly seem to have fallen asleep when I'm woken by a loud bell, like the school bell. The lights are on, but through the frosted window it is still dark. Grandad is down off his bunk, grinning, and pointing at the wall clock, which says half past six. He is stark naked.

I join a long queue, shuffling out of the ward and down the corridor. They are all shapes and sizes and ages but each with the same drooping shoulders and darkened eyes. We go into a large cloakroom, where a matron is handing out uniforms. Soon the room is full of disjointed naked people, changing out of their white clothes and into the familiar red caps, bow-ties, white shirts, and striped aprons of the Burger Cathedral kitchen staff.

A register is taken. We trudge like sleepwalkers out of the main entrance of the Happy House, and are loaded into a fleet of vans marked SICK TRANSIT. I find myself sitting opposite Grandad, who has obviously taken a shine to me.

"Where are we going?" I whisper.

Grandad lifts one side of his backside and unleashes a rasping fart. "Work therapy," he says.

"I don't want to work."

"No work, no breakfast," says Grandad, sitting contentedly in his own foul smell.

Once on Happy Street, the vans divide up, and we are taken to the back entrance of the Burger Cathedral. We stand between two giant industrial dishwashers and wait for our tasks. Some go to the tills, some to the fryers, some to the grills. Some are on drinks, some are on boxing up, some do trays, some stay with the dishwashers. Grandad is put on refuse, and he pulls a few strings so that I get the same.

"They won't put me on the fryers," he says, handing me a broom. "Not enough drive. Lost my drive when they cut out me aggression. See?"

Grandad pushes up his cap to reveal a row of stitches at the top of his skull. A chill runs through me. Grandad, however, seems totally unbothered.

"Quite nice, now," he says. "Nice and calm."

The kitchens of the Cathedral come to life, in an almost military operation. Giant sacks of fries are hoisted out of the freezers, and fork-lift trucks whirr past, loaded six foot high with burgers. Everyone works at the same frantic pace, but with the same vacant expressions. There are targets posted on the wall which we must meet. If we are short one hour, we must make it up the next. Soon I am up to my neck in empty bags and boxes, which I cart out to the bins. Each time I see the bins I see the word REFUSE in bright red, like a taunting message.

"When's the tea-break?" I ask Grandad.

"Hah!"

"No tea-break?"

"Hah!"

"I'm on holiday! This is supposed to be a holiday!"

Grandad beckons me to one side. He leans forward, presses one nostril shut, and snots on to the floor with the other one. Then he changes nostrils. Just as I am beginning to think this was the purpose of luring me over, he whispers, "We're all on holiday. Just like them."

Grandad points through to the servery, and beyond that the restaurant, which is quickly filling with hungry holidaymakers.

"Mind you," says Grandad, "half the others have forgotten. Not me, though. They can't cut that bit out."

"What bit?"

"Me history. They don't know where to find it."

Grandad stabs about his head with his forefinger, then nudges me.

"I know where it is," he says.

"Where?"

Grandad points to his feet. "Down there."

"In your boots?" I ask.

"Lower than that. In me roots."

I look in vain for Grandad's roots.

"You look after your roots," is Grandad's final advice, for the moment.

After four more hours of toil, in which time twelve bins have been filled with various plastic and cardboard junk, the Man arrives. I do not know who the Man is, but he is accompanied by the mind-doctor, and he looks more like a Corpse. He has a grey, papery face, with hooded eyes, and a lipless mouth like a knife-slash. Every few yards, he wipes his finger along a work-surface and inspects the end of it. When he reaches my area, he detects a crisp packet half swept under a freezer. The mind-doctor calls me over and I am sent down on my hands and knees to pull it out. The Corpse keeps his eyes firmly turned away from me. Then he breezes out, with his chest stuck forward like a pigeon, and I spend the rest of the day fuming with hatred and fantasies of revenge. The hungrier I get, the more that hatred grows.

Meanwhile, just ten yards away, the holidaymakers sit behind their fat piles of fried food, laughing and joking and prattling their trivial gossip. Under the stony eyes of the kitchen staff they come and go, following their bloated stomachs in and out of the Cathedral, amongst the endless array of fun and games that is Happy Street.

"Lucky bastards," says Grandad, who seems to know exactly what I'm thinking.

CHAPTER 11

After that first awful day in the Happy House, which seems to last at least a week, I get quite used to the routine. You might almost say it becomes normal. Every morning there is Work Therapy, which lasts twelve hours, followed by so-called "breakfast" at 6 p.m. when a nurse wheels the burgers out of the Food Therapy store, and we all eat like animals. Then there is the Cold Shower, twenty inmates a time, and every day a spotlessly clean white uniform to put on. The day ends with Counselling, which is a bit like a school assembly. The mind-doctor takes Counselling. He says things like "you must learn to tolerate other people's opinions", "you must learn not to be so aggressive", "you must learn not to force your opinions on other people", and "you must learn to fit in with society". Those who insist on still talking about the cliff have electrodes wired to their brains and a burst of five hundred volts put through them.

If we have been especially well-behaved, there is sometimes a Trivia Quiz on our favourite TV stars, known as Soap Therapy.

The Happy House, however, has certain effects on me which are not what the mind-doctor has planned. In the first place, I'm not scared any more. I've been put in the worst place I can think of, and I'm still surviving. Anyway, snivelling into my pillow isn't going to get me anywhere. So I've stopped wishing for Mum and Dad, and started thinking like a criminal, calculating everything. I tell them what they want in

the Counselling sessions, and get away with the mini-
mum amount of work.

In the second place, I've started seeing myself as
part of a team. All the work on Happy Street is done
by inmates of the Happy House, so we have the same
enemies, the same grumbles, and the same desire to
get the hell out of here. There are hundreds of us, and
only a few of them, and it would be so easy to rise up,
overthrow them, and flee back to our fun huts. So
what is stopping us?

The answer is all in the mind. There are many
inmates who have come to believe they really are
mad. Even strong-minded characters have been worn
down by the day-to-day experience of being treated
like an idiot. Other inmates have not decayed quite so
far, but still believe they are capable of nothing other
than the most menial job. These ones tend to be the
sneaks, telling tales on the likes of Grandad and me.
Often they have turned to God, and can be heard in
the Happy House Chapel, singing the McGooey
hymn:

> "He is the rock
> And the solid found–ation!
> He is the rock
> That we build our lives up–on!"

But there is one thing which has a hold on all of
us. Every day, we know there is at least one pleasure
which is guaranteed. It becomes the sole point of
existence. It would be quite reasonable to say that we
are all addicts for the 6 p.m. burger.

With this in mind, one day I hatch a plan. If suc-
cessful, it is guaranteed to have the inmates of Happy
House up in arms. If not ... well, I'd rather not think

about that.

For two days I collect all the paper I can find. This is actually not difficult. We are encouraged to read *The Good News* every day, which is the McGooey daily newspaper. It contains stories of McGooey's successes all over the world, the Burgaball Sports League, the Happy Holiday Smiley Nude Girl, and pictures of Huey McGooey at various charity events with poor blind children and abandoned puppies. It also has the Hot Spots Millionaire Bingo, which I claim to be doing. That is my excuse for sneaking the paper back to my bunk, where I push it firmly under the mattress.

In the dark of night, I begin the slow, patient process of shredding the paper, all apart from one double page, which I roll into a long thin taper. Eventually I have enough for my purposes, at which point I put my fist up to the bunk above and give Grandad a sharp jolt. There is a grunt, then Grandad's head appears, confused but not at all angry, seeing as they've cut that bit of his brain out.

"I need to borrow your lighter," I whisper.

Grandad thinks about this.

"Please," I add.

"Only one I've got," says Grandad.

"I'll get you another one. When we ... escape."

Grandad gets the message. He presses the lighter into my hand, closes my fingers round it, and puts his own finger to his lips.

In the morning, I climb out of bed with six handfuls of shredded paper down the back of my trousers, and the lighter in an even safer place. It is quite common for inmates to shit themselves in the night, and when the assistants see the suspicious bulges beneath my uniform, they think little of it. I wander off pathetically towards the toilets, and they nudge each other and have a laugh.

I am not going to the toilet at all. I make directly for the Food Therapy room, where the burgers are stored. Hastily I feed the shredded paper through the keyhole, poking it down with my finger. I work with incredible precision and efficiency. Soon it is all through, and the only thing left is the taper. I unscrew the lighter and neatly douse the length of the taper in lighter fluid. Then I work the taper through the key-hole, till it makes contact with the floor. It just about gets there, with an inch still showing. I click open the lighter. There is the merest bud of flame left. I apply it to the end of the taper, and hurry innocently on to the cloakrooms to change for work.

All days are bad in the kitchens of the Cathedral, but today happens to be a particularly bad one. There is a run on chicken nuggets, and seventeen kids' par-ties. By the time we get back to the Happy House, we are a mass of burnt and blistered hands, aching feet, griping stomachs and slobbery salivating mouths.

The moment I walk into the canteen, I sense my plan has begun to succeed. There are no trolleys of burgers waiting for us. The mind-doctor and his assis-tants look grave.

The mind-doctor calls for silence.

"No one will eat tonight," he says, weightily.

A hubbub becomes a howling cry.

"No one will eat at all, until we catch the terrorist who set fire to the Food Therapy room!"

There is a moment's silence, broken by a shout of

"Burger!" Others take it up: "Burger!" "Burger!" Never have I seen such anguish. The mind-doctor stands firm.

But the mind-doctor has made a terrible mistake. He holds such control over the minds of the inmates that he cannot imagine them defying him. He does not understand the effect of gnawing hunger. He does not know what that daily burger means to us. He has made no preparations for the riot about to take place.

It is only a matter of minutes before the inmates have smashed their way out of the canteen, down the corridors, through the entrance hall, and out of the main doors. Most head straight for the Burger Cathedral, but a few pathetic characters stay moored to the front doorposts, peering out but terrified to take that first step, like baby birds on their first flight. Others don't even get this far.

Grandad, however, is right at the front of the riot. He is surprisingly sprightly for his age, with a good sense of direction. I run alongside, blithering that it was me who started the fire, hoping the others hear. I want my fair share of the credit.

No one stops us on the way to the Cathedral. In fact, the holidaymakers part and create a channel for us. They have obviously assumed that we are another Save The World charity fun-run, which, in a way, I suppose we are. As we reach the steps of the Cathedral, there is a ripple of polite applause.

That is as far as our good luck goes. We soon discover that all entrances to the Cathedral are closed. The evening shift stand outside, scratching their heads. Word of the food riot has obviously moved faster than we did.

Suddenly I find people turning on me. "He's the one!" they say. "He did it!" For a moment I am afraid my plans will go terribly wrong. But I hold my nerve.

"Yes!" I cry. "Yes, I burnt down the Food Therapy room, and what's more I'm proud of it!"

Gradually all attention focuses on me. I am inspired by blind fear.

"Can't you see?" I cry. "They've got no hold over us now. We're free!"

"But we're hungry!" they cry back.

"Yes! And they'll be hungry soon! When they find there's no one to make the burgers ... no one to serve in the shops ... no one to clean the streets! We'll have them at our mercy!"

"But we're *still hungry*!" comes the cry.

"We can take it! We're used to suffering! They aren't! We'll force them to surrender ... then we'll take over Happy Street ... and have a big feast ... and then ... we will take the building to bits ... and we will *repair the cliff!*"

At the mention of the cliff, the cries of hunger suddenly cease. Everyone seems to snap back to reality. "Ssh!" goes up the call. "Stop stamping your feet! The cliff!"

Fingers to lips, the kitchen staff tiptoe off in search of scraps and a bed for the night, while I return, with gloating satisfaction, to my own fun hut.

CHAPTER 12

"Can I do you now, young sir?"

I jump bolt upright in my bed, with a chair leg in my hand. Mrs D is struggling in with the usual half-ton of gear.

"Mrs D!"

"Had a bad dream, my love?"

I put down the chair leg and retreat under the duvet. Mrs D gathers my dirty clothes in a loving embrace. A warm, secure feeling comes over me, a feeling I had almost forgotten. I close my eyes and begin to drift back to sleep, to the busy, bustling sounds she makes around the room. Then it occurs to me that something is wrong.

"Shouldn't you be on strike?" I ask her.

"Me?" says Mrs D, inspecting my shoes for scuffs. "I've never missed a day's work in my life."

I sit up. "Nobody must work," I declare. "Nobody must work till the Board surrender."

"Oh aye?" says Mrs D, dreamily, giving the toilet bowl a firm squirt of bleach.

"You don't understand, Mrs D – "

"Listen, love," says Mrs D, pointing the bleach at me. "It's my job to look after you, and look after you I will. I can just imagine this place in a couple of days without me. Are you going to keep it clean?"

"I could just leave it."

Mrs D is horrified. "And what do you think would come of that?" she says. "Typhoid, that's what. Typhoid, cholera, and God-knows-what. What would your mum think of that?"

As if to emphasize her words, Mrs D plunges the bog brush down the toilet, attacking the hidden germs that lie round the bend.

"Course, you know who's behind this strike, don't you?" she says.

"Who?" I ask, doubtfully.

Mrs D advances on me, bog brush in hand. "The Martians," she says.

"The Martians?"

"They stir up this trouble ... they watch us collapse ... and the next thing you know ... they're here!"

Mrs D assumes a mask of dramatic and deadly seriousness. Then she gives me a big wink, and I don't know what to make of it.

"Actually," I say, proudly, "I started it."

Mrs D looks doubtful.

"I did, honest. I burnt down the food store. Now there are no burgers left, except the ones they've hidden in the Dallas Fantasy. We're going to starve them out."

Mrs D's great red-cheeked face shakes slowly from side to side.

"But young sir," she says, "what are *you* going to live on?"

"I'll be all right."

Mrs D obviously does not agree. "Just like my lad," she says. "Not the sense he was born with."

"Honest, I'll be all right. I'll get some food off the others."

"You'll be lucky. They'll be looking after number one."

Doubts begin to creep into me. I felt so big when I made that speech last night, but now I am shrinking fast. Mrs D seems to sense it, and tucks me under her powerful arm, like a mother hen gathering a stray chick.

"Don't you worry," she says. "I'll see you all right."

At first sight, not much seems to have changed on Happy Street. Fun buggies still trundle around, kids play in the swimming pools, Huey's face beams down, and the holidaymakers look generally cheerful. I begin seriously to wonder if the strike has taken place at all. Then I notice that the garbage bins seem fuller than usual, and one has actually overflowed. On any normal street this might not seem much, but on Happy Street it is pretty outrageous.

Then I get a real shock. I pass a shop which is closed. All the lights are on, but no one is serving inside, and the door is securely locked. Outside on the pavement, people are buying and selling their own secondhand goods, in a desperate bid to keep shopping. The same scene can be found at the next shop, and the one after that. Everyone seems doubly determined to keep up their way of life, and there is much talk of the Dunkirk Spirit. Radio Happy plays nothing but the new Number One, a disco-funk version of "Keep Right On to the End of the Road", specially recorded by a bunch of soap-operas called the Crazy Rebels.

Beneath the Museum of Princesses, I come across a small food bar which is still open. This is a heavy blow. If someone is betraying us, I want to know who.

I wander in. The place is packed to the rafters with holidaymakers guzzling chips. Toddlers sit on tables and fathers' knees, and older ones sit on the floor. Everyone seems to find this new situation lots of fun. But it is not the Happy House workers who are slaving at the fryers. It is other holidaymakers, obviously volunteers.

For the volunteers, the fun is already wearing off. One has broken her nail, and another is complaining jokily of a headache. As I stand watching, a young lad goes to the counter and orders a burger. The volunteer says there are no burgers, only fries. The lad says he always has a burger. The volunteer replies that she is very sorry, but he will not be having a burger today. The lad demands to know why he won't be having a burger. The smile on the volunteer's face wavers. She asks him politely to go away. He won't. Before my very eyes, the volunteer's expression turns sour. "I don't have to do this, you know!" she suddenly snaps. Instantly the whole café goes silent. The volunteer laughs nervously, and makes a joke of it, but the broadest grin in the room now belongs to me.

Heading off towards the Fanti Arch, I am joined by a small, intense person of about eighteen. He says his name is Neville Greville, and he wants to shake my hand. Vaguely I remember him from my ward in the Happy House. "It's great, what you did," he says. "We'd never have done it without you. Never."

I take it modestly. Neville Greville latches on to me and stays with me half the length of the street. He asks me all about myself and talks excitedly about the escape from the Happy House and my heroic part in it. I begin to understand how Mr Watkins feels when those creeps follow him around the playground, asking him about the time he played for Wales. It's a pain in the arse, but it's a kind of pleasant pain.

"You won't forget me, will you?" says Neville. "When you take over, like?"

Neville waits for my answer with frantic puppydog eagerness. I haven't a clue what he's on about.

"No, sure," I say, just to get rid of him.

Neville pats me on the back. "You're a hero," he says, then wanders off, backwards, giving me a thumbs-up every five yards.

You might think I'm feeling pretty satisfied with myself at this point. But something is bothering me. I'm not sure what it is. Just a sense of something missing.

I check my watch. Six p.m. precisely. Of course. It's time for Food Therapy. Except, today, there won't be any. I trudge back to my hut in a state of utter depression, bordering on desperation.

By the time the sun comes up next morning, I have woken six times and my sheets are soaked in sweat. I don't know if it is hunger, or anxiety, or both together. At any rate, nothing could be more welcome than that rat-tat at the door at 7 a.m.

"Y'all right, love?"

"Um…"

"I've got a little something for you."

My heart leaps. I sit up to watch Mrs D's enormous bum entering the room backwards. She is dragging a picnic hamper behind her. God knows how she lugged it all the way here on her own.

111

"Didn't I say I'd look after you?" she says, between puffs and blows.

"What is it?" I blurt.

With a magician's flourish, Mrs D folds back the top of the hamper. Next second, there in her hand, is the shiny black packet of a McGooey's quarter-pounder.

"Got a microwave, love?" she asks.

"Not with me."

Mrs D winks. "I'll see what I can do."

I crane my neck towards the hamper. "Is it ... full of them?"

"Lord, no," says Mrs D. "If it were full of them, there wouldn't be room for these."

Mrs D holds a bottle of Fanti Cola in the air. I reach out towards it, but she holds it away, and takes out an opener.

"Where did it come from?" I ask.

"Never you mind," says Mrs D. She levers off the cap and pours me a glass, then sits on the bed and offers it to me.

"I'm not sure I should," I say.

Mrs D looks greatly offended. "After all the trouble I've been to?"

"It's just that – "

"You've got to eat and drink, haven't you? What would your mum say if she knew you weren't getting a decent hot meal every day?"

"She'd kill me."

"She'd think she'd brought up a halfwit!"

Mrs D presses the glass of cola into my palm and gently closes my fingers around it. "Don't you worry," she whispers. "It'll be our little secret."

Holiday in Happy Street

* * *

I walk out on Happy Street this bright day in a state of cheery optimism.

"Afternoon!" I call, joyfully, to Mr Braddock next door.

Mr Braddock does not reply.

"How's life?" I ask Jem, from over the road.

Jem dashes a dry bun to the ground.

Decay is setting in fast. Every garbage bin now overflows, and there is a faintly rotten smell of old teabags and orange peel. Fun buggies lie abandoned where they have broken down, with no one to service them. The makeshift shops have given way to a few wide-boys peddling black-market chicken nuggets and bootleg records. In front of the Cathedral is a sign saying CLOSED DUE TO INDUSTRIAL ACTION. THE MANAGEMENT REGRET ANY INCONVENIENCE. Meanwhile, at the first Fanti Arch, the children of the world are kicking the shit out of each other over the last few fries. "Fuck off, it's mine!" can be heard in fifty-three different languages.

Wandering back, later that afternoon, past the Dallas Fantasy, I catch sight of two familiar figures, squatting on the pavement over a gas camping stove. Alice is wearing a brace round her neck and also, for some reason, a sling on her arm and a plaster cast on her foot. Hattie is struggling with a tin opener and a can of beans. She seems familiar with neither.

"*Damn* it!"

Hattie flings the opener to the ground, and at this point notices me.

"Cheer up!" I say. "It's not the end of the world."

Alice and Hattie huddle close together. "You!"

they chorus.

"Got a problem, girls?" I say, with a smile.

Alice's bottom lip droops. "Happy Street was nice before *you* came," she scowls.

"Everyone was quite happy, till *you* came," adds Hattie.

"And *anyway*," says Alice. "You're *dirty*."

"You've got the lergy touch," explains Hattie.

"You came here full of nastiness," says Alice, "and now you've spread it everywhere."

Hattie kicks a broken rattle for emphasis.

"It's you that's being nasty," I say, coolly.

"Exactly!" says Hattie.

"Because you've infected us!" says Alice.

They gather up their camping stove, beans and tin opener, then prance away, noses in the air. They leave behind them a copy of the Happy Street paper, *The Good News*. Feeling a little curious, I pick it up. I am surprised and rather flattered to find my own picture covering half the front page, under a black banner headline: THE KING OF GLOOM. It is the picture from my competition entry form. My eyes have got a mean, hooded squint, but that's because I did the photo in a Woollies photo-booth, and looked straight into the flash.

I read the article with a mixture of horror and fascination. I learn many new things about myself. I learn, for instance, that I am addicted to hard drugs, and have been a petty criminal since the age of six. I learn also that a rival burger chain, possibly Mr Slurpy's, has sent me on a secret mission to bring misery to Happy Street. The article speaks highly of the cheerful, salt-of-the-earth workers of Happy

Street, and how I have forced them to strike against their wishes. It claims that the great majority of these workers are already back at work, and that they are being given all the good jobs. It warns the others that they will be replaced by trained chimpanzees if they do not return within the next two days. Finally, there is a cheery bit about the McGooey Campfire Fun Award, for the best meal made from a can of beans and a camping stove.

A week ago, this kind of thing might have upset me. Now I laugh. But my laughter is cut short as a small pebble zings past my ear. I turn to see Redgrave and Oliver, both close to tears.

"You!" says Redgrave. "*Jesus Christ Superstar*'s been cancelled through you!"

They advance menacingly. I turn and run back towards my hut. This has nothing to do with Redgrave and Oliver, and everything to do with my watch, which has just chimed the magic hour of six p.m.

Mrs D is as good as her word about the microwave. It is waiting for me back at the hut, a beautiful smoked-glass box, the latest technology. I plug it in, then go to the wardrobe where I have stashed the burgers and cola. The burger boxes make two neat skyscraper piles, and it seems almost a shame that I will have to demolish them. The cola crates fit snugly on the other side. My wardrobe is like a well-stuffed stomach which couldn't possibly manage another bite.

I select one box, and one bottle, then retire to the armchair to study the instructions.

The box to a McGooey's burger is a work of art.

On a black gloss background sit the simple words "one McGooey's quarter-pounder", and a devastating photo of the goods inside, clear in every detail, with the pale bun pulled back to show the glistening slab of pure beef, its relish gently oozing. With trembling fingers, I prise open the box, and there it is. I lift it out as carefully as a little sleeping hamster. I carry it on its paper napkin over to the microwave, open the black smoked-glass door, and feed it in. With the merest brush of a finger on the touch-sensitive controls, the burger begins slowly to turn, displaying itself from all angles before my hungry eyes.

There is a noise outside. I jump quickly to the door, and check again that it is firmly locked.

Now for a cola. I take the bottle in one hand, and snap the cap back with the other. There is a crack, and a fizz, and a little cloud, like a smoking gun. Meanwhile the microwave has given a musical Ting! and my meal is now complete. I lay it all out before me, peel the napkin from the burger, and say a short prayer of thankfulness to Mrs D. Next second I am gorging myself, in a feast of squelching luxury.

After it is over, I flop back in the chair, full to bursting. Suddenly I am overcome with a terrible feeling of guilt. I jump up, seize the burger box, curse it, and hurry to the toilet. I tear the box into tiny, tiny scraps, fling them down, and flush them away, followed by the screwed-up napkin. I drop the empty cola bottle back in its crate, and shut tight the wardrobe door. Never again, I say to myself. Never again.

CHAPTER 13

The Good News has done me a real favour by making me the front page story. All the workers have united behind me. If you back the strike, that means you back me. No one dares criticize me. If anyone says I'm only a kid, or I'm just in it for myself, five hundred people leap to my defence, and say I'm a great lad and twice as mature as my age.

This has a big effect on me. I want to live up to it. If they ask me questions, I want to give them answers. Overnight I become an expert on anything and everything. I nod my head, stroke my chin, and give intelligent, mature opinions, even if I know sod all about the subject.

"Ben," they say, "we're going to stick posters up. What shall we put on them?"

"Hmm," I reply. "That's a tough one. How about that photo from *The Good News*?"

"Ben," they say, "how long are the Board going to hold out?"

"Hmm," I reply. "Depending on the weather … twelve to thirteen days."

Neville Greville appoints himself as my messenger, rushing everywhere with my words of wisdom. I say something one minute, and it's done the next. It's like having a thousand hands.

But as time wears on, uncertainty grows about what is happening and what is going to happen. The air is thick with plots and counter-plots and strange deeds in the dark of night. One evening a group of workers uncover a secret store of cola in the toilets of the Burger Cathedral. As I arrive, they are smashing bottles into the beautiful glass of the Cathedral windows. They then begin to push the piles of crates down the Cathedral steps, with bottles and cans smashing across the courtyard, and howls of anguish from the holidaymakers. The workers respond with more crates and screams of hatred against McGooey's. Soon a clear brown river of cola is streaming across the courtyard, through Fanti Cola Arch, and onwards down Happy Street. People fling themselves on to their stomachs, mouths open, to swallow what they can of the flood. Kids scrap over the few dented cans that survive. Grown men and women push each other aside like firsties in the dinner queue. I stand there transfixed, with the cola lapping around my socks, thrilled and terrified.

There is a voice in my ear: "Ey up, Crackpot."

I turn to find Becky, standing alongside me, hands on hips.

"Y'all right then, Loony?" I reply.

"Not so bad."

We refocus on the action on the Cathedral steps.

"Told you I'd make them listen, didn't I?" I say, smugly.

"You're my hero," says Becky.

"I've started a revolution."

"Started a riot, more like."

"Same thing."

"It is not! Look at them! They should be saving the cola, instead of smashing it up. No one knows what they're doing. Nothing's organized. You got no plan of action."

Becky stabs a finger in the general direction of the Dallas Fantasy. *"They're* organized... They've got their food supplies ... they've got their propaganda ... they've probably already infiltrated us with spies."

I turn to her. "'Us', is it now?"

"Yeah. Course."

"Well, *you* go and stop them then," I say, triumphantly.

Becky considers a while.

"All right, then," she replies.

I stroll away. The last I see of Becky, she is wading into the flood, both arms raised, yelling "Stop!"

CHAPTER 14

I should have thrown out all the burgers after that first one. The more the days go by, the less likely it is that I'll ever break the habit. But there is no point in feeling guilty about it. Fifty burgers won't go far between all those workers. Anyway, my well-being is vital to the success of the strike. I've got to stay healthy and optimistic, or the others will lose heart.

I have developed a daily routine which never varies. At around 5.30 p.m. I get the first pangs and start making my way back to my hut. At 6 p.m. on the dot, I click open the wardrobe door. Burger in the microwave, check the door is locked. First swig of cola, three inches left to help the burger down, one more inch left for after. Tear up the napkin and burger box, flush down the toilet. Empty bottle back in the wardrobe.

None of this is done in a frenzy. It is done calmly and systematically. I go about the process like a true professional, then sit back and relax, in the satisfaction of a job well done. No one will ever know, except Mrs D of course, and it's all right her knowing.

The next time I see Becky, she is pushing a metal wheely-bin down the middle of Happy Street, with half a dozen others around her, carrying sacks.

They are walking through a scene of utter devastation. The rubbish is now piled ten foot high, almost as high as the stink it gives off. The neon lights on the

Fanti ads blink and flicker, sometimes reading FA–T, sometimes –ANTI, sometimes FA–TI. The swimming pools are filled with stagnant green algae and floating cans. The ice rink has turned into a field of churning brown sludge. Graffiti covers the Video Supermart. Barbed wire surrounds the holidaymakers' huts. People skulk in the shadows, heads down, like animals hunting. Kids fight off the seagulls for the last remaining scraps of burger bun. The pictures of Huey hang broken and crooked, in a mass of dead and twisted neon, like something out of Becky's paintings. Posters of me are plastered tauntingly on the walls of the Dallas Fantasy. Many have been savagely ripped, and on one, the eyes have been gouged by angry fingernails.

I run my own fingers, reassuringly, over my real eyes. Then I stuff my hands in my pockets, whistling casually, and saunter up to Becky.

"What's going on, then?" I ask.

"Ey up, Ben. Meet the Food Committee."

The others smile eagerly.

"Great, isn't it?" says Becky, indicating the surrounding wastes. "Makes me really happy, seeing the street like this. This is how it ought to look. Like what it really is."

"What's the Food Committee?" I ask, anxiously.

"Told you, it's us. We were elected by the others. Weren't you at the general meeting, yesterday?"

"When was it?"

"6 p.m."

"No ... must've been somewhere else."

"We're doing brilliant. We've got hold of all this cornmeal. Everyone's meeting at the Distant Star

121

tonight, and we're going to cook it up in these bins, and share it out. The Entertainments Committee is organizing some music. Come up! All you need is a bowl."

"No one told me about any of this," I mumble.

"Ben, you don't own this strike, you know."

"Never said that."

"There's only one thing that matters, and that's winning."

"I know that."

"Come up tonight, then. People'll want to see your face."

"I'll see."

I don't know why it bothers me so much, other people taking over like this. Still, I say to myself, I'm more of a figurehead, like the Queen.

I am almost home from my afternoon stroll, when I notice the Braddock's little girl watching me. I have avoided my neighbours since Mrs Braddock said she was praying for my sickness to be healed. Nevertheless, I give the little girl a wave. She darts back indoors. There is much squawking, then a slap, and Mr Braddock hastily closes the door.

It is now that I notice that my own door is ever-so-slightly open. I move warily. I peer in through the door, and gently press.

It all happens very quickly. Something massive comes down, cudgels the floor, and leaves a blinding pain in my pointy finger. When I have recovered my senses and sucked hard on my poor digit, I realize that a boulder of sandstone rock has missed me by maybe two inches. Now it lies there on the floor, sunk into its own crater. That crater might have been in the middle of my skull.

Even after all my experiences, the closeness of death comes as a real shock. For a while I sit down, one hand to my frail head, watching the other hand quivering of its own accord. Out in the courtyard, a Funbulance draws up. Two capped heads look round, see me, and drive on again. The silence returns, and by now, even silence is sinister.

I stand up on two jelly legs, and, with all the strength I have left, lift the boulder. Staggering like Frankenstein's monster, I lug the evidence down to the Laughing Police Station.

Several changes have taken place at the station. For instance, a small video camera follows my progress to the front door. Inside, there is a high metal grille above the counter, and the old brass bell has been replaced by an electric buzzer.

No one answers the buzz. With great difficulty, I climb under the counter, pull back the curtain, and make a dramatic entrance into the back room. The Laughing Police are obviously taken unawares. The Admiral is inspecting his face in a silver dustbin lid, and the Bosun is encouraging Flossie to sink her teeth into the oven glove on his hand.

"Someone," I pronounce, "has just tried to kill me."

The Admiral lays down his dustbin lid.

"If it isn't our young friend," he says.

"Someone," I repeat, "has just tried to kill me."

The Admiral holds up his hands.

"Let's find the Incident Book, shall we?" he says.

The Admiral begins sorting through his desk with

tortoise slowness. After a couple of minutes he finds a large blue book, and begins thumbing steadily through the pages.

"Lost Bicycles... Cats in Trees... Jammed Locks... What was the problem again?"

"Someone," I repeat, "has just tried to kill me."

The Admiral raises his eyebrows.

"With this," I add, thrusting forward the sandstone boulder.

"Hmm," says the Admiral, tapping it with his pen. "Could do some nasty damage, a thing like that."

"In the wrong hands," adds the Bosun.

I lumber the boulder on to a nearby chair and start gabbling.

"I opened me door and it just come – "

"Wo, wo, wo," says the Admiral, holding up his hands.

The Admiral applies his pen to the Incident Book.

"I ... opened ... my ... door..." he repeats, carving the words slowly on to the paper, "and ... it ... just ... came..."

"And it just come down SMASH, and made this massive hole in the floor, and winged my finger. Look."

The Admiral takes little interest in my bruised pointy finger. He begins slowly to repeat the second half of my sentence, then thinks better of it.

"I thought you said someone tried to kill you, sir?" he says, looking up.

"That's what I'm describing."

"Aren't you being just a little ... *paranoid*, sir?"

"I'm not paranoid."

"It seems to me, sir, the whole thing could just as

124

easily be an accident."

"An accident?"

"Don't you ever leave things around, sir, and forget where you've put them? I certainly do. Pens...
Incident Books..."

"Not on top of doors."

"Not normally, sir, but there was that time when I
was wallpapering the ceiling – "

"Excuse me. But surely it is obvious to anyone of
an IQ of five that someone is trying to kill me."

A new mood comes over the Laughing Police. The
Admiral lays down his pen. The Bosun takes his hand
from Flossie's mouth.

"Are you casting aspersions as to our IQ?" asks the
Admiral, solemnly.

"No. I mean..."

"I think we should look at this from another
angle."

Suddenly I'm blinded. There is an anglepoise lamp
blazing into my face, and the Laughing Police have
become looming shadows behind it.

"Well have it your way, sir," says the Admiral.
"We'll assume that somebody is trying to kill you.
That suit you, sir?"

"Could you just ... turn that light down a bit?"

"Let's build up a picture, sir, of the kind of person
who would want to commit such a foul and senseless
deed. Any ideas, Bosun?"

"I fancy an ... ordinary kind of chap," says the
Bosun.

"I'll go along with that, Bosun. Someone with a
simple, perhaps old-fashioned sense of right and
wrong."

"Rather like us, Admiral?"

"You might say that, Bosun. You might say that!"

"I think our chap's confused, Admiral. He looks around, and what does he see? Chaos, where once there was order. Criminal acts going unpunished. He feels the need to take action."

"An understandable feeling, Bosun. An entirely understandable feeling. He has his wife and family to protect."

"Exactly, Admiral. From rioters … hooligans … lunatics wandering the streets…"

"He wants a broom, Bosun. A big, big broom, to brush them all away."

"Get them, Admiral, before they get him."

"But wait, Bosun. There are so many of them. Things have gone so far. If only he could find the *root* of the evil…"

"And *cut it out!*"

The Bosun draws a sharp finger across his own throat.

"I'm sorry, sir," says the Admiral. "Did you say the light was too bright?"

"It's … in my eyes…"

"The light of truth, sir? The light of truth too bright for you?"

"Please … I want protection."

"Hmm," says the Admiral.

"Hmm," says the Bosun.

"You're the police. It's your job."

"Is that so?" says the Admiral.

"First he questions our IQ," says the Bosun, "now he tells us our job."

There is a long silence.

126

"You will of course have to sign the Protection Form," says the Admiral.

"You mean you'll protect me?"

"If you sign the form, sir, certainly."

"Where is it? I'll sign now."

The Admiral takes a neatly folded sheet from his top pocket, and carefully smoothes it out on the desk. It says:

I CONFESS TO BEING AN AGENT FOR MR SLURPY'S.

I push the paper away. "I can't sign this."

The Admiral lets out a weary sigh. "If only young people would help the police," he says, "the police would be more than willing to help them."

He refolds the Protection Form and pockets it. Meanwhile the Bosun is plugging in a bright new jug kettle and sorting out two cups.

"What am I going to do?" I plead.

The Bosun hands me a bent teaspoon. "Best we can offer, I'm afraid, sir."

The Laughing Police adopt sad and sorry expressions. I pocket the puny spoon. The Bosun moves the curtain aside for me. With light-spots before my eyes, feeling faintly sick, I make my way out.

"Oh, and one last thing, sir," says the Admiral.

"Uh?"

"Don't go using that spoon as an offensive weapon, sir. Criminal offence, sir."

I am blown out on a gale of gusty laughter, which echoes in my head, long after I have escaped the station.

CHAPTER 15

My close escape from death has shaken me into a new life, more urgent and fantastic than anything I could have imagined. I stand before the mirror in my room looking at a stranger. His eyes blaze with life. His skin is flushed with blood. His nostrils drink deep of the air. His mouth aches for food.

I go to the wardrobe with one thought in mind: survival. I go through my precious rituals with no apologies, and no hesitations. Does a lion say sorry when he sinks his teeth into the neck of an antelope? Does he doubt for one second what he must do?

Afterwards, I flop gratefully into the cushions of my chair, like Dracula, refuelled, with the tang of blood still on my lips.

There is a knock at my door.

"Yes?"

"Ben?"

I feel for a weapon, but find only my teaspoon. "Who's that?"

"Becky. Open up, will you?"

I unlock the door. Becky lets out a huge sigh of relief.

"What's the matter?" I ask.

"I thought you were dead," says Becky. As if to reassure herself that I'm not, she puts a hand on my arm. I look down on it. A new feeling has come over me. A lioness has strayed into my lair.

"Came back, didn't I?" I reply.

Becky takes her hand away. I back into the room. Becky comes in, uncertainly, and stands just a few feet inside my territory. I casually point out the boulder crater, and my injured finger, and make as little of it as possible. I so wish I'd brought back the boulder, so I could make little of that as well.

Becky relives it all with me. Her face grows angry. It is as if we are being drawn closer and closer together. I look into her face and realize I've never really looked at her before. I've always thought she was quite ugly, but the details of her eyes and mouth are almost beautiful. I move towards her.

"We've got to go," she says.

"Why?"

"Everyone's got to see you."

"Now?"

"Yeah, now. They're up at the stadium."

"They can wait, can't they?"

"They're going crazy! They think you're dead!"

For some stupid reason, Becky now decides she needs a long stick. I tell her I haven't got one. She clicks her fingers and says "clothes rail". Next second, to my horror, she is heading straight for the wardrobe door.

"Get out of there!" I yell, barging her aside, and flattening myself against the door.

"What d'you do that for?"

"That's my bloody private wardrobe!"

"That's no reason to push me!"

"How'd you like it if I went through yours?"

"Suit yourself, mate. Everyone else has."

"Well mine's private!"

"Lucky you."

We stand eye to eye, in a poisonous silence. Eventually Becky says "Forget it", and stomps off to the door, where she waits impatiently for me to follow. I slouch after her as slow as I can.

I discover that Becky hasn't come alone. There are three fun buggies parked outside my hut, and three staff in each, armed with rounders bats. When they see me they cheer. They all want to touch me, shake my hand, slap my back, as if to check I really am alive. Becky watches in a sullen sulk, as I wallow in the attention.

The fun buggies set off, a fairy-lit motorcade, towards the Distant Star Stadium. Along Happy Street there are small groups of holidaymakers, bags packed, trooping back towards the railway station. If the holidaymakers are leaving, then victory is surely not far away.

We're still outside the stadium when we reach the back of what seems an enormous crowd. The woman in the front seat of my buggy sends businesslike messages down a walkie-talkie. At the other end of the walkie-talkie I can hear chanting in the background. At first it sounds like "Buns! Buns!" but as we get closer I realize it is "Ben! Ben!" I sit up, and pull my shoulders back.

"Can you hear that?" asks the guy next to me.

"Sure," I reply coolly.

The motorcade turns into the stadium. No Olympic marathon winner has heard a greater roar. Every single worker on Happy Street must be in that stadium, together with all those holidaymakers who have come over to our side. The crowd stretches out on all sides in a vast village of makeshift tents, lit by a thousand torches. In each corner of the village is a bonfire, and on each bonfire a refuse bin, used as a cooking-pot. From the state of the faces as we pass, it is clearly the first meal they have eaten for a long time. Their cheeks are drawn in and their eyes are hollow. Yet there is something about them so immensely strong and dignified, that they seem to be burning some secret fuel. I am more than ever convinced that these people will never give in.

The motorcade draws up at the stage. The staff form a guard around me, and I am bustled up the steps, into the spotlight, like a championship boxer. Without thinking, I raise my arms, and am astonished at the wild response it brings. I do it again.

There is a DJ at the mike. He silences the crowd.

"You see this man?" he says. "This is the man they said was dead! Look at him! Does this man look dead? Comrades, they *cannot* kill him! This man is bulletproof! Comrades, I give you … the *great* … Ben Lewis!"

Many things go through my mind as I take that microphone. Some are simple things, like whether I should call the crowd "ladies and gentlemen", or "comrades" or "brothers and sisters". I wonder how many people are out there. I think of the girls that must be watching.

Deeper than this, I feel an overpowering sense of destiny. A sense that somehow this was all meant to happen, that I have been chosen to play this part, that history is unfolding according to some great plan. From the corner of my eye I see myself projected fifty feet high on the video screens. I fist the sky and shout, "Yeah!"

"Yeah!"

"Yeah!"

"Yeah!"

An incredible exhilaration runs through me. This is it, the thing we all dream of, the thing we play-act every day in the school playground. This is glory.

"They said I was dead!" I cry. "Do I look dead?"

"No-o-o!"

"They can't kill me!" I cry. "I'm bulletproof!"

"Ye-e-ah!"

My blood courses. I am so wildly excited, I think I'm going to take off. The DJ approaches the mike and I flap him away impatiently. I'm not finished yet.

"They said we were mad!" I yell. "Are we mad?"

"No-o-o!"

"Who's mad?"

"They are!"

I thrust my pointy finger into the air, and gabble furiously about the murder attempt, and the Laughing Police, and how this is the wound, this is the proof. In the midst of the cheering, I drop on to one knee, aim my wounded finger into the audience, and clamp the other hand to my wrist, like a police marksmen. Slowly I level it round the huge anonymous crowd. I'm ready for you, if you're out there! You just try it again, and see what happens!

Many hours after, when the night has cooled, I sit alone on the edge of the stage, faintly glowing from the bonfires that still burn around the stadium. Nearby, a group of staff work out a rota of body-guards to protect me. Beside the nearest fire, Grandad sits with his arm round an equally old woman, both

132

eating hungrily from makeshift bowls. Everywhere there is the same air of fellowship and optimism, and people talk of the good times to come, when it is all over, when we all own the street together, and the cliff is once more safe.

I am woken from my own dreams to realize that Grandad's new friend is standing before me, with a plastic bowl of yellow porridge in her hands. She offers it up to me. Her hands and her face are wrinkled, and yet she looks eager, and playful.

"Take it," she says.

"No, no, it's all right. You have it."

"I want you to have it," she says. "Please. Please share in our meal."

"No, really."

She gives me no choice. She will not be satisfied till the bowl is in my lap and the spoon is in my hand. She returns to Grandad only when I have taken my first tentative sip and told her how good it is.

At this point I notice Becky, wandering off towards the stadium exit. "Hey!" I shout, and run after her.

She turns.

"Want this?" I ask, offering her the bowl.

"No thank you," she says, coldly.

"What's the matter with you?"

"What d'you think?"

Becky folds her arms and views me critically.

"Oh, that!" I go. "You ain't still going on about *that!*"

Becky sniffs and looks away.

"You ain't still going on about *that!*" I repeat, nudging her with the porridge bowl.

"Don't touch me," says Becky, eyes flashing me from top to toe.

There is an action replay of our earlier poisonous silence, but that was then, and this is now.

"I'll touch who I bloody well want," I tell her.

CHAPTER 16

Dear Mum + Dad
    Sorry I haven't written for
a few weeks but quite a lot has
happened. I went down the beach
and after that they sent a sick-
ologist to see me. They locked me
up in a mental home but don't
worry, I escaped from there and
started a Rebellion. Someone
tried to kill me but don't worry
its only because I'm so famous now.
Anyway now we've won. Tomorrow
we are going for talks with the
people who run Happy Street, and
then we will take it over and
stop it collapsing into the sea.
    Give my love to Gran.
        Love, Ben R. Lewis

Mr + Mrs Lewis
137 Goldacre,
Milton Keynes
Bucks
ENGLAND

The news of surrender was brought by one of the
lesser members of the Board. He was a pathetic char-
acter. His suit obviously hadn't been cleaned since
the laundry closed down, and his face was scarred in
the big punch-up that had broken out over the last
burger. He gabbled about the cliff, and how it wasn't
his fault, and how he'd known all along Happy Street
couldn't be built that way, and how impossible it was
to argue when everyone was so scared for their jobs. I
watched his bulging bloodshot eyes without pity. I
told him a few home truths about the Happy House,
and what it was like on the other side of the fryers. I
told him he'd get his just desserts, like the others.

The public meeting is set for 5 p.m., in the Historic
Council Chamber. Grandad remembers when the
Historic Council Chamber was built. Like the rest of
Happy Street, it isn't historic at all, but once it was
used in a TV movie about George Washington.

There is a big debate as to whether we should have a leader at this meeting. Many are against it, but obviously someone has to draw up a Surrender Document and the terms for our takeover. Anyway, it doesn't mean they're in charge. They're just, you know, the leader.

I argue strongly for having a leader. "Have you anyone in mind?" they ask me. "No, not at all," I reply. "What about you?" someone says. "Me?" I reply. "Well, I don't know about that…" "Go on, Ben!" they all cry. "Oh, all right then," I reply.

It is a great privilege and responsibility. I therefore dress up in the suit Mum and Dad bought me last Christmas, and spend some time making fine adjustments to it in the mirror. I trim my hair and gel it back. I practise some politician poses. Then I tear a sheet out of my school exercise book and write out the Terms of Surrender:

TERMS OF SURRENDER

We, the undersigned members of the Board, do Hereby Declare:

① All claims concerning the state of the cliff are true.

② We renounce ownership of the street, which will pass to the former inmates of the Happy House

③ We are very sorry. We intend to grovel for mercy at the feet of Mr B. Lewis, esq.

As we will be going to the Historic Council Chamber, I yellow the document over a candle, and burn round the edges, like those treasure maps we used to make. At 5 p.m. precisely, it is in my black briefcase, heading into the Dallas Fantasy. My bodyguards follow, heads up, walking through those great doors with the pride of kings and queens.

The scene inside the Dallas Fantasy is one of unthinkable decay. There is a foul smell of nylon-shirted armpits and blocked drains. Clouds of dust fly up from our tramping feet. The trees and plants are yellow and withered. Paper planes, cigar butts and bun-crumbs litter every desk top and windowsill. The great bronze letters are tarnished black, and graffiti covers the walls. Now that the Board are powerless, they have taken to spraying McGOOEY'S RULE over everything in sight.

In the centre of this miserable mess, waiting to greet us, is an equally miserable person. His face is lifeless, his shoulders hunched. He wears a second-hand Oxfam suit, several sizes too small. His beer gut spills out through his buttonless shirt. From the bottoms of his trouser legs run varicose veins, wandering about his skinny white shins like trails of lumpy blue porridge. He breathes short and shallow, and by the way he staggers towards us he is clearly drunk.

"This way," he says, trying to lay a hand on my arm.

"I can manage thank you," I reply, moving away.

"Ben, you've got to understand – " he babbles.

"Shut up, DT," I snap.

It is as if all the energy and confidence has been drained out of DT and injected into me. I brush him aside, and with generous arms, guide my own party forward.

"I wouldn't get too cocky, y'little bastard!" yells DT, just like the alkies when you won't give them 10p.

Fifty paces on, we make our historic entry into the Historic Council Chamber. It is an awe-inspiring moment. The Historic Council Chamber is shaped like a bull-ring, seats rising on all sides, and every single inhabitant of Happy Street waiting. In the centre of the ring stands the McGooey Chair, embroidered in red and gold, with crown and coat-of-arms. It stands above the famous crystal case containing the fossilized remains of the first ever McGooey's burger. Before it is an antique desk, not much wider than a chess board, and on the other side of that is a simple little chair, a school chair.

At first I do not recognize the man who sits in the McGooey chair. But as he turns to watch our progress into the room, memories of the Cathedral flood back to me. This is the man I named the Corpse, that pompous, mean-mouthed supervisor who did his best to humiliate me in the Cathedral kitchens. I hold up my hand, and halt my posse.

"Where is Huey McGooey?" I ask, and my voice echoes grandly around the oak panels.

The Corpse's knife-slash mouth parts barely a millimetre. "He is watching you right now."

"Where?" I ask, looking round.

"No matter," he says. "He is with us."

I walk down the steps, in silence, to enter the arena, alone. With a quick glance to the audience, I run my finger along the desk and inspect the end of it. The Corpse makes no reaction as I display the dust to him.

"What's this?" I say, giving the school chair a little kick.

"I'm awfully sorry. The other chairs were destroyed during the *strike*."

He pronouces the word "strike" with distaste and contempt. I am not afraid of him, but I cannot help feeling a twinge of admiration. He shows such class in the face of defeat. And like me, he has risen to the top. He is a leader. I can learn from him.

"Well, young man," he says. "Have you a speech prepared?"

I decide to remain standing. I take my time, spotting the familiar faces in the audience, just to show who's boss. I begin to speak, without notes. "Many weeks ago," I say, "when I first came to Happy Street…"

I retell the whole story, of the beach, the cliff, the lies, the injustice, the attempt on my life. The more I speak, the more confident I become, and the more confident I become, the more authority there is in my voice. I add new details to the story, amazing myself with the same spell that amazes my audience. I thump my fist to emphasize a point, and it works, so I do it again. I wag my finger sternly, and shake my head gravely, and open my arms wide in an appeal to my people. My speech reaches a triumphant crescendo, in which I hardly know what I am saying. Members of the crowd rise to their feet, applauding wildly, while I cough into my hand, in a terrible attack of modesty. Finally I drop into my seat, forgetting it is a school chair, and suddenly find myself looking up into the stone face of the Corpse, utterly unmoved.

I take the Terms of Surrender from my pocket and

slam them forcefully on to the desk between us.

The Corpse takes out a pair of half-glasses, puts them on, and studies the paper at arm's length. The crowd settles.

"We seem to be at cross purposes," he says, finally.

"What's wrong with it?" I snap.

"It is you who has come here to surrender," he pronounces.

In the stunned silence that follows, the Corpse draws his own papers from an inner pocket.

"First of all," he pronounces, "can I assure all the workers of Happy Street that their jobs are still open to them … with the exception of those who have been involved in terrorist activities, such as the destruction of property."

"What you talking about?" I blurt.

"I regret that you have been drawn into this long, painful and unnecessary strike, which has done so much harm to the friendly, peaceful atmosphere of Happy Street."

"Don't listen to him!" I shout, rising to my feet.

The Corpse lances me with a rigid stare.

"This little boy," he says, "has led you a merry dance. He has watched you suffer, in pursuit of his own ends. This whole charade is the result of his own selfish ambitions."

"That's a lie!" I shout.

The Corpse rises, more than a foot above me, and points into my face.

"This boy," he pronounces, "has a four-foot pile of McGooey's burgers in his wardrobe."

My heart drops to my boots. There are gasps on all sides.

"Perhaps you'd like to deny it," adds the Corpse, with a cruel, twisted smile.

There are urgent calls from my supporters to make the denial.

"Yeah," I blubber. "Yeah, I do deny it."

The Corpse withdraws his finger, takes a few calm breaths, and turns to his side. There in the front row, rising to her feet, is the plump, matronly figure of Mrs D.

"He's lying," she says.

It is as if my own mother has stood up in court to give evidence against me. I am devastated.

Mrs D continues. "He's got, oo, thirty burgers, I'd say. He's eaten the rest, of course. Along with the cola. I know, because I clean his room. I've been cleaning it for him all the way through the strike. A proper Little Lord Fauntleroy."

There is more urgent advice from my supporters: "Say something, Ben!" "Deny it, Ben!" But my hands and feet are prickling and my face is as hot as a coal fire. "It's all true," says Mrs D, turning from one side to the other, amidst the turmoil.

Suddenly there is a new voice in the crowd. "Why should we believe you, you bloody scab?"

Grandad! Grandad has spoken!

"Who said that?" says Mrs D, furious.

"I did!" says Grandad.

"Well, you're a foul-mouthed, dirty old man."

"Better than being an arse-licker," says Grandad.

Mrs D gasps. Grandad appeals to the crowd in general. "A week ago they said he was an agent of Mr Slurpy's. Then they told us he was dead. They'll say anything."

141

There are cheers of support. The workers begin to mock Mrs D, and laugh at the idea of my secret supply. Soon I too am mocking this ridiculous notion.

"Ben wouldn't eat a McGooey's to save his life!" someone shouts.

"Hear, hear," cry the workers, and I smile.

"Ben's the only honest person on Happy Street!" someone else shouts.

"Hear, hear," cry the workers and my smile broadens.

"Go and look in the bloody wardrobe, if you don't believe it!" shouts a third voice.

"Hear, hear," cry the workers, and my smile becomes a false and rather sickly one.

At last everybody in the chamber, except me, agree on something. An inquiry team will be sent to my hut, the wardrobe will be opened, and the truth will be established beyond dispute. I desperately try to think of one good reason why it shouldn't happen, but my own supporters are all for it, and my mind is a blank. The inquiry team get set to leave.

"Um..." I blurt, "how do we know we can believe them?"

My point is taken. The Corpse declares that we may have our own witness on the team. I suggest me. It is decided that this is not really on. Then someone suggests Becky. Who better? say the others.

At 5.40 p.m., amidst excited whispers, Becky and the inquiry team depart the chamber, leaving the rest of us to sit tight and await their findings.

I am surprisingly calm. There are well-wishers on all sides of me, and they have such faith, that I have a growing feeling I will miraculously escape. I assure everybody that the worst thing the inquiry will find is my dirty socks, and each time I say it, I believe it more. I am Ben Lewis, practically a legend, and you cannot destroy a legend.

Fate. Fate will intervene. A tribe of mice will have carried off the burgers and left no evidence. It is all part of the great plot I have been playing out.

Five fifty-five p.m. The doors to the Historic Council Chamber burst open. The inquiry team have returned, carrying several Video-Mart plastic bags. To cries of dismay, they empty the bags on to the oaken floorboards. Cola bottles and burger boxes rain down in an endless stream.

"It's a plant!" someone shouts.

"He's been fitted up by the Laughing Police!" another cries.

"Becky!" cries a third. "Tell us the truth, Becky!"

Becky has entered the chamber last. She is white-faced and drawn. There is an eerie silence as her wounded eyes meet mine. Her lip quivers.

"Judas," she says.

Slowly, painfully, she draws the sleek black box of a McGooey's burger from her pocket, and drops it to the ground.

There are howls of anguish. I leap to my feet, pointing deliriously at Becky.

"You don't believe *her*, do you? She's mad! She's totally bloody mad!"

CHAPTER 17

Dear Mum + Dad,
   Coming home immediately.
No time to explain. If
you don't see me by
tomorrow, ~~get the police~~
~~write to the papers~~
~~tell the government~~
come and find me!
      Love,
      Ben

Mr + Mrs Lewis,
137 Goldacre
Milton Keynes
Bucks
ENGLAND

I hurriedly pack my bags, stuffing toothbrushes, presents and pyjamas any-which-way, and prepare to
make my escape from Happy Street. Outside there is
the constant churn of cement-mixers, and clank of
scaffolding, and tramp of feet. The McGooey hymn is
on everyone's lips:

"He is the rock
And our solid found–ation!
He is the rock
That we build our lives up–on!"

The song is now compulsory. Happy Street is in a
reign of terror. Miserable faces are no longer tolerat-
ed. Pessimism is no longer allowed. Fainthearts and
doubters are treated with scorn. Happy Street is building again, with wondrous new structures appearing in
all corners, taller and bolder and more colourful than
ever before. Any staff who resist are mysteriously
disappearing. The others trample over each other in
their efforts to carry as much stone as possible,

because there is a bounty on each stone, and the chance of getting rich.

Everywhere, on leaflets, flags, trailed through the sky by aeroplanes, is one slogan: WHAT IS GOOD FOR McGOOEY'S IS GOOD FOR YOU.

It is as if McGooey's is a tree that we have been pulling and pulling, trying to break, and now it has snapped back the other way, with more force than ever before.

I sling my bags over my shoulder, and put on a single-minded money-crazed grin, so as to look inconspicious. Then I slip out into the night, sprinting between the shadows. I am heading for Becky's hut, to grovel in apology. She is probably the only one person who knows how to get out of here.

It is incredible how much building has already been completed. Not far from my hut is a sign advertising a new shopping mall and multi-cinema complex to be completed by Tuesday, and next to that work has begun on the Dallas Fantasy Space Research Centre and Charity Shop. Men in red, blue and green hard hats swarm over the scaffolding like ants, hauling up the new blocks of sandstone which are piled according to colour. Meanwhile a stream of fun buggies bear down on the Cathedral with a constant supply of burgers and cola.

I am sure everyone is looking at me suspiciously. But then, I am probably looking at them suspiciously. Everybody is looking at everybody suspiciously. You never know who's after your sandstone blocks.

I scamper quickly down a side-alley and, gasping for breath, arrive at Becky's door.

I knock. "Becky?"

No answer.

"Becky, it's Ben!"

No answer.

I try the door. It opens. I creep inside. The room is much as it was before. The mug of tea I never drank still sits on the floor, gathering mould. But her drawings have gone, and her sleeping-bag, and her old rucksack. I wander round the remains, stupidly, then sink down in the cushionless chair with my head in my hands.

She can't have gone. She can't. She's a girl. Girls are supposed to care. She *knows* I don't know the way out.

I sit in that chair for a long, long time, confident that door will swing open, and she'll appear, and give me that weary look, then say "Come on then". It doesn't happen. Gradually I begin to accept the impossible. She has abandoned me.

I go back into the night with a terrible sense of dread, made even worse by the fixed smiles and unwavering sense of purpose all round me. I have hardly set two feet back on Happy Street when a hand lands Clunk! on my shoulder, and I find myself looking up to a red-hat.

"Come on, son," he says. "Tea-break's over."

"I'm too young to work," I plead.

"Too young to work, sir."

"Sir."

"Then why aren't you on a Scheme?"

"What kind of a scheme?"

"A youth-draining scheme, of course."

"Please," I plead, "just leave me alone."

"Roy!" the red-hat man calls to his mate. "We've

146

got a scrounger!"

His mate, another red-hat, comes over and views me like a dog. I am sure I've seen him before. Apart from the little macho moustache, he bears an uncanny resemblance to my number one fan, Neville Greville.

"Please," I whimper, "I just want to go home."

"We all want to get home, mate," says the first red-hat.

They take an arm each, with hands like vices, and frogmarch me down Happy Street. People wish them a good evening as they pass, and several congratulate them on catching Another One. We eventually halt at a sign saying YOUTH-DRAINING CENTRE.

"This," says the first red-hat, "is where you learn the meaning of Duty."

I am guided into a circle of youths, who kneel round a hurricane lamp, watched over by an old schoolmistress at a high Victorian desk and chair. Clearly the youths have already been drained of all enthusiasm, energy and curiosity. Number one is holding a roller skate without wheels, and with a rusty screwdriver fits wheels to the front half. Number two then takes the skate, and fits wheels to the back half. The skate goes on to number three, who spins both pairs of wheels and inspects the screws. He hands it to number four who, with great care and precision, removes the back wheels. Finally the skate goes to number five, who removes the front wheels and hands it back to number one.

I am given the job of number three, who is sent off to the youth-draining college to write an essay about the usefulness of his experiences. I receive training in the form of a clip round the ear from the old schoolmistress and a boot up the backside from the red-hats, who then go off in search of other scroungers.

"What's your name then?" I ask number two.

"Ssh!" says number two, handing me the skate, with an anxious glance at the schoolmistress.

It does not take me long to pick up the skills. I spin the wheels backhand, and forehand, with one finger, and with two. I close one eye, then both eyes. Soon I have forgotten what it was like not to spin wheels. I spin wheels without even knowing I am spinning wheels.

The others show no desire to escape. Some of them are perhaps older than me, yet I feel ten years older than all of them. They seem to accept the situation, but I can never accept it. They think this is just the way it is, but I know how different it could have been. Worst of all, I know whose fault it is.

"Careful!" comes an urgent whisper.

I realize I am banging so hard on the wheels, they are practically buckling. My finger bleeds. Good, let it bleed.

I stop spinning the wheels. Number four holds out her hand. I ignore it. Number four looks anxious. I lean forward and casually strap the skate to my left foot. Number four's eyes pop.

Number one hastily gets to work on another skate. I take a glance at the schoolmistress. She is wrapped up with *History of McGooey International, Vols I - IV*.

Number two takes the skate, and fits the back wheels. All eyes are on me as I casually check the screws, fit the skate to my right foot, and climb awkwardly to my feet.

"See you folks!"

With a quick burst of acceleration I am past the old schoolmistress and on my way down Happy Street. Behind me I hear shrill shrieks of "Stop him!", overcome by shouts of "Go!" from the drainees. Soon I am overtaking the fun buggies, and thwacking redhats to the ground as I pass. I sail past the burger stalls and the building-sites, faster and faster, faster than a downhill dream. I swing round the lamp-posts to change direction, and tuck in like a skier to cut down the drag. All the boredom and frustration of the youth-draining centre has been transferred into forward motion. Forward, past the Dallas Fantasy. Forward, past the Fame School. Forward, past the Porcelain Fountain. And now, the right fork, the fork of freedom, and no one within a mile of me.

Here I am in unknown territory. I skate serenely round a bend in the road, hoping maybe to see a motorway sign, or an ordinary village, or at worst, an open road.

What I find instead is a fence. A massive electrified fence, bearing the sign DANGER – END OF THE FREE WORLD. I do not know if it means that the Free World is this side, or that side, or just ended.

Across the road is a checkpoint. Not a grey miserable one, but a bright, polka dot cabin, with Radio Happy blaring, and roses round the door. From this cabin emerge two dark figures, with mirror-visors over their faces, and dustbin lids in their hands. Between them is a large slavering hound, who drops into a sinister nose-down prowl at the sight of me.

I stay very still.

"Identification?" says the first figure.

"Haven't got any."

"All hooligans carry identification," says the second figure.

"I'm not a hooligan."

"How old are you?" says the first figure.

"Fifteen."

"Just as I said," says the second figure. "A hooligan."

"Identification please," says the first, holding out a hand.

I make no move. The hound's hindquarters quiver. As it readies itself to pounce and tear my arm off, my mind flashes back to an old leather-top desk, and immediately I recognize the dog.

"Flossie!"

The dog pauses.

"Admiral!" says the second figure. "Did you hear that? He called our dog Flossie!"

"Criminal offence, Bosun," says the first. "Get him, Fang!"

In the confusion that follows, I lose two inches of best denim from my jeans, while Flossie and the Laughing Police end up in a frantic pile of swinging arms and swear words. I find myself skating through a dense thicket of trees and brambles. The brambles catch in my skates and I am dragged slower and slower, almost to a standstill. I splash into a stream, scramble up a mudbank with my wheels skidding uselessly, then plunge into a sea of ferns. But nothing will throw Flossie's nose off the scent, and her barks are closing in, along with yells which would fill the station swear box a hundred times over.

At last there is daylight through the trees. I find myself facing a long, low, featureless building. The white building. It was a mystery when I was on the Big Wheel, and it is a mystery even now, just yards away. I feel down the walls to a pair of plain white doors, then yank frenziedly at the handle. After half a minute of pulling with all my might, I push instead. The doors come straight open, and I tumble in. Into what, I do not know.

There is a switch on the wall. I try it. Fluorescent striplights flicker on, bright, white, and cold. The room is maybe fifty foot square, with shiny white-tiled walls and a concrete floor. There are low walls, like a maze, but where they lead I don't know. In the air there is an antispetic smell, but the antiseptic covers something else, something potent and rancid.

Flossie's angry barking is very near. I press myself back to the wall, praying she'll go past the doors. In my haste I have left them open a few inches, but there is nothing I can do about it now.

My prayers are not answered. The barks become wildly excited as Flossie reaches the doors. There is a scrabbling of claws, and next second, the dog's head appears through the opening. I hold my breath. Flossie sniffs the air. She gives a low, unearthly whine. Then she backs out of the room, and runs for it, fast, with yelps of fear.

I feel no relief. A chill runs through me. Something has happened in this place. Something terrible.

All my senses are alive, watching, listening, tasting the air, trying desperately to find out what Flossie knew all too well. Outside, the Laughing Police arrive, shouting for their dog, but getting no response. Their voices become low and urgent as they conspire their next move.

I stay low, gliding behind the low walls towards the heart of the maze. The smell seems to be getting stronger. And the stronger the smell, the more anti-septic. White channels appear beside me, like urinals. Then a drain. Everything is spotlessly clean. I cannot understand how so much cleaning has failed to get rid of that bloody smell.

The Laughing Police fall silent.

Something is about to happen.

I move on, with every creak of my skates sounding like an orchestra. I am getting close to the heart. I turn one corner, then another, and this one is the last.

At this point, I discover I am not alone.

Before my eyes, rising and falling, squeaking faintly, are a pair of size 15 shoes, maroon with yellow spots.

Trousers, like billowing chessboard tents.

Spinning bow-tie.

The face of Huey McGooey.

But no laughter on this face. Just the thin, sadistic, knife-slash mouth of the Corpse. It opens, like a wound, to reveal a small row of shark-teeth.

"Ben," it begins, in the voice of the Corpse. "How good of you to come!" it adds, in the voice of Huey.

The famous clown opens a hand sticky with blood, and offers it to me. I back off in horror. He laughs, and with a bloody finger paints a broad red smile around his knife-slash mouth.

Suddenly there is a crash, a massive BANG, and choking grey smoke everywhere. Smoke-bomb. I am

152

stone deaf. Everything has suddenly become a silent movie, with the Laughing Police looming through the smoke in black balaclavas, and Huey grabbing me by the collar, mouth opening and closing soundlessly. Violently I wrench myself away and smash through the nearest doors, smack into the lolling body of a cow, its throat slit and a river of blood streaming from the gaping cavity.

My live hands rattle at the next door, a great weighty bolt, which gives way into a new silent nightmare, a frozen world of hanging corpses, banging into my face as I skid and slide idiotically past. It is a forest of death, nothing on all sides but more cold bodies, swinging slowly from their unexpected meeting with me, like some dumb dancers, legs stretching hopefully back to earth.

Another door, another bolt. I break out of the cold into a cavernous barn, with a warm, live, shitty smell in the air. Round the sides of this barn are rows of metal half-doors, like starting stalls. Inside the stalls are live cows, packed so tight they cannot turn, but face the wall like naughty children, hopelessly casting their big tennis-ball eyes back towards me. I release the bolt on the nearest stall. A huge, steaming beast staggers out backwards, on spastic legs. I skate on to a second stall, then a third, pulling bolt after bolt, with half-terrified animals shambling out behind me, baffled by the freedom. Gradually they form a ramshackle herd, going one way then the other, like a shoal of fish. I cower away from the silent trampling hooves, and skate for my life to the far end of the barn, where a corrugated door stretches from floor to ceiling. Only now do I realize it is electrically operated. I press myself into the corner, terrified, as the ramshackle herd becomes one great stampede, and a thunderous noise comes up in my ears, like the volume on a TV being turned slowly to maximum.

The Laughing Police tumble from the cold-store door, and draw back in fear. Through the noise and dust I see them battering furiously on the door that has closed behind them. Now they are trapped like me. How strange, I think to myself, that it should end like this. Trampled into 100% peopleburgers.

But there is at least one chapter to come. The door is beginning to open, rising from the ground in a juddering motion. Gradually the feet, legs, chessboard suit and bloody hands of Huey McGooey are revealed on the other side.

Too late, Huey realizes what he has unleashed. In blind panic he turns and flees. The terrified mooing horde spill out after him, a river of flesh, the weight of a battleship. I take my chance and skate for my life behind.

In no time the stampede has wiped out six tennis courts and a statue park. They funnel into an alley, heading straight for the street itself. For a brief second, I catch sight of Huey, hands up, a pleading expression on his face. Then he has gone.

I hear the shrieks of the others long before I reach Happy Street. By now the head of the stampede is far in the distance, and even Radio Happy cannot blot out the noises of devastation as it sweeps on, through the Fanti Cola Arch, past the Dallas Fantasy, on towards the Porcelain Fountain. Cows rampage through the market stalls, splash into the swimming pools and plough down the decorations, running on

154

with trails of fairylights round their necks. Scaffolding shudders, the ground trembles, and little cracks appear between my fleeing feet. I scream at the youth-drainees to run for it, and some do, but others are hypnotized, like rabbits. On and on go the herd, past the Fame School and the fun huts, crushing everything flat, like a path to freedom. Past the Porcelain Fountain, now a pile of broken dishes, on to the checkpoint, snapped like a matchstick by the weight of the teeming herd. I scream noiselessly at the others to hurry, hurry, hurry. Suddenly there is an enormous aching groan deep beneath the ground, closely followed by a noise which turns the whole stampede into no more than a whisper in a library. The unthinkable has happened.

CHAPTER 18

The odd thing about the survivors of the Great Collapse is that they show nothing. They do not throw their arms round each other. They do not beat the ground in anguish, or wail for their lost children, or cry thanks to heaven for their salvation. They walk. We all do. Some walk down the road. Some walk back towards the ruins. Some take the path by an old canal. Some overtake me, silently, then a few minutes later pass by, the other way. It is a perfect, clear day, a perfect English landscape, but somewhere on the other side of the universe.

I arrive at a railway station. It has white palings and red begonias in hanging baskets. On Platform One, upon a plain green bench, sits a crumpled figure in an old overcoat and flat hat. I cannot imagine why Becky is still around, nor what coincidence led me to find her. I sit down, a few feet away, and she does not acknowledge me, and we say nothing.

At length a train arrives. It is a small train, just a couple of carriages, some of British Rail's old stock. Becky gets into the front carriage and I follow. We sit at separate ends. I run my hand along the string baggage racks, the dirty metal ashtrays, the broken blind, and the gum pressed into the groove beneath the window. There is a jerk, an easing of brakes, and we move off, past fields dotted with sheep, a square church tower, the Red Lion, and cooling towers on the horizon.

The guard comes in, grey-faced, wasted, dark

round the eyes. I hear myself saying: "Single to Milton Keynes, please."

The guard's hand comes up from his ticket machine, and floats like a leaf up to his mouth. Something is worrying him.

"Milton Keynes, please," I repeat.

"No," says the guard, in a faint croak, shaking his head.

"What's the matter?"

"But ... haven't you heard?"

"Heard what?"

"You really don't know?"

"Don't know what?"

The guard looks slowly down to his stomach, then gives his ticket machine a little tap. A long green stream of tickets spews out, like a paper intestine. He carefully separates it from himself and walks away, leaving it coiled on the floor.

I pick it up. I turn it over. There is nothing on it, either side.

My fingers clench into the arm of the seat. There is no feeling in them. I run them up my arm, and across my chest, but there is no feeling there, either.

The train to nowhere clatters steadily on, clicking across the rails. Click... click... click...

click...

click...

click...

"Damn and blast," says a voice, a voice from nowhere, the voice of Leon's uncle. "Damn and blast, I can't get him back."

GATE-CRASHING THE
DREAM PARTY
Alison Leonard

"And everyone famous was there – the Queen
dragging Princess Anne in a pushchair, Paul
McCartney looking like Lady Macbeth in a pink
bikini. And I was the engine of it all. It was a
merry-go-round with me as the central pole…"

When Robina flunks her GCSEs, she decides
there's only one thing to do – leave home. So, with
a barrel-bag containing a few essentials (top of
which is the written record of her dreams) she sets
off for Bristol. Over the next few days she
encounters so much that's strange she often finds
it difficult to distinguish dream from reality.
Strangest of all is Vern, the taciturn, infuriating
youth she teams up with… Has Bina just run from
one nightmare into another?

DEEP HOLY JOE AND THE
BALLAD OF THE BAND
Michael Gizzie

All night long the bands went on and off.
The judges were smiles and laughs,
marking points and signing autographs.
Holy Joe watched the faces.
The last chord of the last band died.
He watched his band take their places,
and went alongside.
The band took the stage...

In a suburb, somewhere, five school leavers form a band: Sam, the strummer; Mike, the drummer; Ace, the singer; "Brass-Finger" Bob on sax and Itchy Fred on keyboards. Holding them together is Deep Holy Joe, bassist and guru. This colourful blues ballad is their story.

THE SECRET LINE
William Corlett

Neither black nor white, Jo Carson feels ill at ease
in her skin. But then Mit, a longlost childhood
friend appears and takes her to the Secret Line – a
mysterious section of the Underground with
stations such as Heath, where she meets the
engaging runaway David. But further down the
line, at Jungle, danger lurks in the shape of the
vicious thug Straker...

"Most interesting and most ambitious."
The Observer

GEOFFREY'S FIRST
Jon Blake

Today is the birthday of Geoffrey Stratfield
Farmer – prig, snob, know-it-all and self-elected
future Conservative Prime Minister. But it's also
the day on which Kim McConnell – TV starlet,
fledgling *femme fatale* and Geoffrey's classroom
rival – is back at school. Which means that
Geoffrey's in for some hard lessons about life in
general – and sex in particular...

"A funny and moving love story... Geoffrey is an
excellent creation. He is extremely funny."
The Sunday Times

MORE WALKER PAPERBACKS

For You to Enjoy